D0344650

Emily Windsnap
and the
Ship of Lost Souls

Also by Liz Kessler

Emily Windsnap
and the
Ship of Lost Souls

LIZ KESSLER

illustrations by SARAH GIBB and NATACHA LEDWIDGE

CANDLEWICK PRESS

Text copyright © 2015 by Liz Kessler
Illustrations copyright © 2015 by Sarah Gibb
Text break illustrations copyright © 2012 by Natacha Ledwidge

First published in Great Britain in 2015 by Orion Children's Books,
a division of the Orion Publishing Group

First U.S. edition 2015

Library of Congress Catalog Card Number 2015936355
ISBN 978-0-7636-7688-9

15 16 17 18 19 20 BVG 10 9 8 7 6 5 4 3 2 1

Printed in Berryville, VA, U.S.A.

This book was typeset in Bembo.

Candlewick Press
99 Dover Street
Somerville, Massachusetts 02144

visit us at www.candlewick.com

This book is dedicated to someone who was a friend and a wonderful artist, and who respected and loved the sea more than most.

"Every given moment passes only once, colours are constantly evolving, but the relationship between the sea and the land is eternal."

Lucie Bray, 1974–2014

Behold her on the silent sea,
Yon vessel like a spirit there!

Moved in a dream's reality,
As if she trod the air.

None can tell from what creek or bay
She sailed out, or by night or day;

They watch her like a vision gone
Over the sea's oblivion.

from "The Ghost Ship,"
by Robert Crawford

Chapter One

An exciting Invitation from Fivebays Island

*E*ighth grade. Week two. Assignment one. *What I did over summer vacation.*

I chewed the end of my pen and tried to think of something I could say that wouldn't make Mr. Rollins, my new English teacher, think I'd made it up.

I had the feeling that if I wrote *I went on vacation to an ice-filled land where I found people's lost memories in a magical pool, helped unfreeze Neptune's evil brother, turned him into a mountain, and ultimately saved the future of the world,* it might come back with *FAIL!*

This is supposed to be fact, not fiction, scrawled across it in red pen.

So I decided to write about my birthday instead. I had turned thirteen on September 4, just before we came back to school. Yes, I know, I look much younger. I'm the oldest in my class and the smallest as well. Which is kind of weird. Not half as weird as everything else about me, though. And this last year was a bit different from usual, what with discovering I was a mermaid, freeing my dad from a prison out at sea, nearly getting squeezed to death by a sea monster, and having about a million adventures in the ocean. Oh, and getting a boyfriend!

All of which meant that by the time my birthday came around, I was *more* than ready to celebrate.

I set to work writing about my birthday party and wondering what I would be doing if I were at Shiprock Mermaid School right then, instead of Brightport High.

Since we had come back to Brightport, my parents and I had spent weeks discussing how my schooling was going to work. When you're half human and half mermaid, decisions like these are trickier than they are for most people.

We finally came up with an answer just before the school year started. The deal was that I'd go to "normal" school (Mom's word, not mine. Mom's the full-time human in the family) from Monday to Thursday. And because "nothing much of any use ever seems to happen at that school on Fridays" (Dad's phrase, not mine. He's the merman, and the one who'd like me to be learning siren songs and ocean rhythms every day), I would go to mermaid school on Fridays and Saturdays. Shiprock has school on Saturday mornings, so at least I'd get a couple of days a week there.

It wasn't the perfect solution, but it was keeping the three of us happy for now. At least, Mom and Dad were happy. I wasn't so sure about myself. Every time I sat in class doing things like writing essays about what I'd done over summer vacation, I wished I was with my best friend—and full-time mermaid—Shona, learning about sirens and shipwrecks, or how to make a trampoline out of fishing rope, or the hundred other things that I learned out in the ocean.

Trouble was, when I was at Shiprock, I spent half my time worrying about what I was missing at Brightport! Mandy Rushton—my onetime enemy, now a good friend—always filled me in, but it wasn't the same. See, Dad was right. Nothing much of any use ever *did* happen on Fridays, but it *was* when people had the most fun.

Whichever way I looked at it, it seemed I was missing out. The only silver lining was that because Aaron, my boyfriend, is a semi-mer like me, he had the same arrangement. Which meant that he was in the same place as I was, no matter which day of the week it was. And I had to admit, that mostly made all of it better.

"OK, folks, class is almost over, so finish the sentence you're writing and put your pens down." Mr. Rollins shuffled papers around on his desk while he waited to get everyone's attention.

A second later, the bell rang. Mr. Rollins called over the noise of chairs scraping on the floor, "Chairs behind your desks, and don't forget your homework. Oh, and there's a letter for each of you to take home to your parents. Please pick up an envelope on your way out of the classroom."

"What's this about?" Mandy mumbled as we collected our letters. The envelopes were sealed, so we couldn't see what was in them. On the front, they just said, *To the parents of Brightport High eighth-graders.* On the back, each was labeled with the words *An exciting invitation from Fivebays Island.*

As I read the words, I felt a funny sensation inside me — like a tail swishing around in my stomach.

I had mixed feelings when it came to islands.

On the one hand, an island, by definition, is surrounded by sea — which is totally fantastic, obviously, as it generally means lots of opportunities for the mermaid part of me to go out exploring in the ocean. On the other hand, I'd had some of the worst experiences of my life on an island, including nearly being squeezed to death by a sea monster — which isn't as much fun.

4

"'Fivebays Island,'" Mandy read aloud. "Sounds cool."

And as I pocketed my letter, I had to agree. All things considered, Fivebays Island sounded *very* cool.

I forgot about the letter for the rest of the day. It was only once I got home and was unpacking my bag that I remembered it.

"Oh, Mom, Dad, this is for you," I said, passing it over to Mom.

Mom took the letter from me and reached for her glasses as Dad popped his head up from below deck.

We lived on a boat moored in Brightport Harbor. It was a beautiful old ship that had been specially adapted so merpeople and humans could both live in it.

"Hey, little 'un, how was school?" Dad asked, flicking wet hair off his face and smiling up at me. I took my shoes and socks off and sat on the edge of the gap in the floor, dangling my feet in the water. Just my toes, so my legs wouldn't turn into a tail. Part of the new deal was that I had to do my homework before going in the water.

I shrugged. "OK." I nodded over to the table,

where Mom had opened the envelope and was now sitting reading the letter. "We were given those."

Dad looked over. "What is it?"

"Emily's class has been invited to visit an island for a geography field trip at the end of this month," Mom replied.

I was emptying my bag of all the junk I'd accumulated through the day, but my heart thumped down on the table along with my browning apple core. So it was just a geography field trip. The dullest thing in the world.

"They'll be studying rare birds and exotic plants and unusual geological formations," Mom went on. Then she looked across at us and added, "It's for a whole week."

I dropped my homework planner on the table with a thud. A whole week studying birds, plants, and rocks? *Really?*

"Oh, and there are shipwrecks and some interesting sea life, too," Mom went on. "They'll organize glass-bottom boat trips."

Shipwrecks and sea life? That sounded much better! But they could forget the glass-bottom boat trips. If shipwrecks and sea life were in the cards, I wanted to go underwater and see them up close!

"I think she should go," Dad said.

"Me too," Mom added.

"Yeah, I think so too," I agreed. If my record with

islands was anything to go by—who knew?—
perhaps I'd find myself caught up in an adventure
while I was there!

That evening, Aaron and I swam out to Rainbow
Rocks to meet up with Shona and Seth.

Seth is Shona's boyfriend. Well, she hasn't officially
called him her boyfriend yet—but I know she'd
like to. They met in the summer when he helped
us save Neptune from his evil twin. As a thank-
you, Neptune made him one of his advisers. He's
only fourteen, so he's the youngest merboy ever to
hold such a high position. But it means he doesn't
get to hang out with us all that often, as he's pretty
much at Neptune's beck and call. Luckily he had
the evening off and could join us.

Swimming over to meet them with Aaron, I
forgot all about school and geography field trips.
When I was in the water, everything else floated
away. Nothing that happened at Brightport High
could ever come close to the feeling of zooming
along, racing a shoal of tiny bright-blue fish, or
darting in and out of coral and rocks, or gliding
along on a warm current, holding Aaron's hand.

When we arrived at Rainbow Rocks, Shona

waved us over and pulled me in for an excited hug. Seth and Aaron greeted each other with more boy-like greetings—i.e., a grunt and a nod.

"The *best* thing happened today. I've been dying to tell you!" Shona squealed.

"You got the highest score on the B and D test?" I ventured. Beauty and Deportment is Shona's favorite subject. It's all about sitting correctly on rocks and brushing your hair smoothly while singing siren songs at a perfect pitch. I'm not very good at it, myself. It always feels a bit like that game where you have to rub your tummy and pat your head at the same time. I've never been any good at that, either.

"No. Well, yes, I did, actually," Shona said, blushing a little. "But it's not that."

"Mrs. Sharktail accidentally put her skirt on backward?" Aaron offered. Mrs. Sharktail is the principal at Shiprock School, and ever since embarrassing Aaron and me in front of the whole school for being semi-mers, she hasn't been on our list of favorite people.

Seth laughed. "That would be funny," he said.

Shona was getting impatient. "I'll tell you. It's a geography reef trip! It's in a few weeks. We're going to study shipwrecks and sea life and—"

"Is it at Fivebays Island?" I asked.

"Yes! How did you know? I asked if you could

8

come, but Mr. Finsplash said he doesn't think you'll be allowed because you have to attend full-time and—"

"I'm going!" I squealed.

"We both are," Aaron added.

Shona stared at us both. "You are? But how come? Mr. Finsplash said—"

"We're going with Brightport High. I'm guessing it's the same week!" I grinned. "They must have sent letters to both schools at the same time."

Shona grinned back. "Swishy!" She jumped so high, her tail came out of the water. "Oh, it's going to be such fun. Mr. Finsplash says the island has a shallow reef all the way around it. There are *loads* of amazing rock formations, and there are shipwrecks and hundreds of varieties of fish that you don't get anywhere else. And guess how it got its name."

Aaron scratched his chin and scowled, as if thinking hard. "Hmmm, I'm going out on a fin here, but does the island by any chance have five bays?"

"Yes!" Shona glanced at Aaron and realized he was laughing. "Oh," she said, flicking water at him. "Well, OK, I suppose that might have been obvious."

"It sounds swishy," Seth said with a shy smile. He didn't strike me as the kind of boy who would normally use Shona's favorite word, *swishy*, to describe something fun. I guessed that meant he was *definitely* her boyfriend. "Wish I could join you."

"Maybe you could ask Neptune for a few days off," Aaron suggested.

"That would be super-swishy!" Shona exclaimed, clapping her hands so excitedly she splashed seawater in my face. Then she turned as red as a snapper fish and tried—belatedly—to look unconcerned. "That's if, you know, you want to," she added with a shrug.

Seth smiled. "I'd love to," he said. "I'll try. But you know Neptune."

Oh, yes. *I* knew Neptune. Probably better than any of them. The king of all the oceans was not someone you mess around with or someone who granted favors lightly. I'd been on his wrong side often enough to know that.

"I'll give it a try," Seth said again. Then he reached out to take Shona's hand. "It would be great to spend the week with you guys."

Shona beamed as brightly as the multicolored rocks behind her. "Come on," she said, swimming away—presumably before Seth could see that her face had turned even redder. "Let's go to the playground. Some netting floated in the other day, and I've started making a trampoline."

We followed Shona through the water. As I swam, I thought about the upcoming trip. I was looking forward to a simple week away with my friends, with no drama. No frozen people. No sea monsters. No prisons guarded by hammerhead sharks.

Just a nice, normal week — with maybe the tiniest adventure thrown in for a bit of excitement.

Whatever else happened, I was determined that my trip to Fivebays Island would be free from *anything* weird and scary.

Not that it was up to me, of course.

Chapter Two

September passed quickly, and it wasn't long before I was packing a bag and getting ready to join my classmates for the mammoth journey. It was Saturday morning, and a bus was picking us up at noon to take us on a five-hour drive up the coast, followed by a four-hour crossing on a boat over to Fivebays Island. With any luck, we'd be there before nightfall.

I squashed my last bits and pieces into my bag and pulled the zipper shut.

"You've packed all your geography books and your binoculars for the birds, haven't you?" Mom asked.

"Yes, Mom."

"And the charts I gave you so you can recognize and record all the fish?" Dad added.

"Yep."

Mom held her arms out. "I'm going to miss you, sweet pea," she said as I hugged her.

Dad leaned on the trapdoor and reached up to kiss me on the cheek. "Me too, little 'un."

I wasn't sure if they should really still be calling me things like *sweet pea* and *little 'un* now that I'd turned thirteen, but since I was leaving them for a week, and since every other time I'd left them recently, my life had been in danger from either a kraken, an evil ice man, or an ancient curse, I decided to let them off the hook.

Clutching my bag, I stepped off the boat and made my way along the wooden jetty that led up to the pier.

"Hey, Emily!" A voice called from ahead of me.

It was Mandy. I waved at her. "Wait for me!"

As we made our way up the pier, I could see the group of children waiting. There were only twelve of us on the trip; not everyone had chosen to come. And about the same number again would be coming from Shiprock. Plus, there'd be a teacher from each school.

A flicker of excitement went through me. We'd had another letter last week, telling us what to expect. It was from someone named Lowenna Waters. Which I'd thought was a joke name at first. I mean, she's in charge of an island and she's named Waters? That'd be like a math teacher named Mrs. Multiplication. But it had turned out to be real.

Lowenna's letter said that she and her husband, Lyle, looked after the island. No one really lived there apart from them — it was one of those places that were kept free from human interference so they could protect all the varieties of animals and birds that live there. Their job was to keep it that way, and to educate people about all the things that they protected.

Lowenna said that she would organize games and trips and we'd have loads of fun, as well as learn more about geography than you could ever learn in a classroom. She'd written to Shiprock School, too. Shona showed me her letter. It included information about shipwreck tours and sightseeing trips to underwater places that hardly anyone has ever seen before.

Both letters said how proud they were to be hosting the first ever joint trip between a human school and a mer school.

I couldn't wait to get there.

"OK, eighth-graders, listen carefully," Miss Platt, our geography teacher, called over the din as the boat drew toward Fivebays Island. We'd been traveling all day and were pretty tired, but the sounds of anchors grinding against metal and engines changing gear as we docked in the harbor was enough to reawaken our excitement.

From the front deck of the boat, I stared into the twilight of the early evening to try to catch a first glimpse of the island.

"When we arrive, we will be greeted by Mr. and Mrs. Waters. Please be on your best behavior. They have worked extremely hard to provide an exciting week for you and have promised us a wonderful welcome, so can we ensure that we all show them the utmost respect at all times?"

We all dutifully did the "Yes, Miss Platt" thing as we jostled for the best spots at the front of the boat. I really wanted to dive off the boat and swim up to the shore — but I had the feeling that might not fit in with the "best behavior" promise, so I stood and waited with everybody else.

Eventually, the boat's engines died, the gangplank at the front came up, and we were herded into the semidarkness of Fivebays Harbor—which might be a bit of a grand thing to call something that seemed to consist of a jetty only just large enough to fit our boat alongside it, a scrappy beach covered in stones and stranded seaweed, and a couple of rowboats tied up on big round buoys at the other end of the beach. Was this supposed to be one of the wonderful five bays?

"Hmm. Right. Now, then," Miss Platt mumbled as she pulled a folder out of her bag and started rifling through papers. "Mrs. Waters said she would be here to meet us."

We all peered into the gloom. There was no one around, and no sign that anyone had been around anytime recently, either. Just us, the beach, and the soft waves lapping gently over the rocky bay. I wandered down to the water's edge. The stones jangled as each wave came in, hissed as each one retreated.

Over on the other side of the bay, Miss Platt was walking this way and that, waving her arms around and checking her phone for a signal.

"What do you think is going on?" Aaron was by my side.

"No idea. Maybe they've forgotten us." We stood in silence for a moment, mesmerized by the rhythm and the tunes of the waves.

Mandy came over to join us. "Miss Platt is talking to someone now. I think they're on their way."

A few minutes later, a shadow came across the

beach. As the shadow got closer, I could see it was a tall man, quite gangly, with wavy hair that flopped around all over his head as he hurried toward us. His shirt was half hanging out of his pants, and his face was covered in dark stubble.

"Nice to see he's made an effort for us," Mandy mumbled.

The man headed over to Miss Platt. "I'm so sorry to keep you, Mrs. . . . er . . ."

"Miss Platt," Miss Platt said, holding out an arm to shake his hand. "No harm done. You're here now."

"Yes, yes, of course," the man said. He turned to go back up the beach and indicated for us to follow. "Well, I'm Lyle. My wife is, er . . . Look, sorry we kept you. Anyway, come on, then. I'll take you to your cabin."

Putting it politely, the man seemed completely clueless. He didn't tell us anything about the week ahead or ask us if we'd had a good journey, or, well, anything. He didn't talk. He just walked, and we followed, shuffling along the sand with our bags, and up the slope at the top that took us onto a path through a small woods. For a few minutes among the trees, it was virtually pitch-black.

"Careful in here; it's very dark," Miss Platt called back, pointing out the obvious. "Keep an eye on the person in front of you and stay close together."

Aaron grabbed my hand.

"Any excuse," I joked. Not that I minded.

The path through the woods led to a dirt trail with a couple of houses. One on the left of the trail, and one farther up on the right. "This is the island's main road," Lyle said. "And that's your cabin," he added, pointing to the house to our left. When we got to the door, he rummaged in a pocket for a key and let us in.

"You've eaten?" he asked.

"Yes, thank you," Miss Platt replied. "We had dinner on the boat."

"Good." After fumbling around on the wall for a light switch, Lyle gestured down the corridor. "Bathrooms are down there. Kitchen is all the way to the end and around the corner. Living room is the room after that," he said hurriedly. "Bedrooms are all upstairs. Boys in the rooms on the left, girls on the right. The teacher's room is at the end. Make yourselves at home. Any questions?"

We stared at him. Was that it? That was our "wonderful welcome"?

Miss Platt shook herself. "Er . . . What time would you like to meet us in the morning?"

"Meet you?" Lyle replied. He was already halfway out of the door.

"Yes, for our . . . Hold on a sec"—Miss Platt rummaged in her bag and pulled out a sheet of paper—"Island Intros and Official Orientation," she said, passing the paper to Lyle.

For a split second, his face softened into a slight

smile. "Lowenna and her funny titles. Always with the alliteration," he said, almost to himself. He passed the sheet of paper back to Miss Platt.

"Look, I'm sorry you haven't had quite the welcome you were expecting," he said. "Things have been a bit . . . Well, look, we'll sort it all out in the morning, OK? I'll come over at nine and we'll get together in the living room and take it from there. Is that all right?"

"Well, I suppose so," Miss Platt replied tightly.

"It'll have to be, won't it?" Mandy whispered in my ear.

"All right, then. Have a good night," Lyle said, and, with that, he left us standing in the corridor and closed the door behind him.

Miss Platt took a second to get herself together before regaining her normal teacherly tone. "All right, children, let's get settled. Take your things up to the bedrooms and we'll meet in the living room for hot chocolate in ten minutes. How does that sound?"

It *sounded* great. Only trouble was, it didn't work out to be quite so good. For one thing, the beds were all unmade and we had to spend fifteen minutes searching all the rooms and cupboards for sheets and blankets.

Half an hour later, when we'd made the beds, we were more than ready for a cup of cocoa with warm milk. But there was no cocoa. Or milk.

Miss Platt sighed as she pulled a loose strand of hair back into her ponytail. "I think we should call it a night," she said. "I'm sure everything will feel much better after a good night's sleep. Set your alarms, children. At eight thirty, I want to see you all down here for breakfast."

Breakfast? With no milk?

"I'm sure they'll have figured something out for us by then," she added quickly.

We headed for our rooms and said good night.

"Sweet dreams," Aaron whispered as we parted company in the corridor. I wanted to give him a kiss, but I made do with a quick smile and a "'Night, sweet dreams," back at him.

Five minutes later, I was in bed and fast asleep. It had been a long day.

Lyle seemed to have gotten his act together a bit the next morning. He was there at nine, like he'd said. He'd even managed to find some milk and bread for us. No butter, but we had jam and peanut butter and even half a box of Frosted Flakes to share. He talked while we finished off our breakfast.

"I hope you all had a good night's sleep," he began. "First of all, may I apologize again for the rather disorganized welcome last night? It's not how we normally like to welcome our visitors. The thing is, well, um . . ." He paused and looked away from us. Then he shook his head. "You see, my wife organizes these trips and, unfortunately, she's, er . . . she's had to go away."

"Lowenna's not here?" Miss Platt broke in.

"Um, no. She says she's really sorry and—"

"But she organized the whole thing."

Lyle frowned. "Yes. I know."

"She said that she would personally supervise us, show us around, give us games to play, bring the two classes together." Miss Platt started rummaging in her bag again.

"Look, there's no need for that." Lyle waved her paperwork away as if it were a wasp. "I know this isn't quite what you expected, but it will have to do. I'm sorry. It was . . . it was unavoidable." His eyes looked dark as he spoke, and his voice had turned a shade sharper. What was going on here? What had happened to Lowenna?

Miss Platt put the papers back in her bag and sat up straighter. "All right, then," she said tightly. "What *will* my children be doing today? Lowenna said there would be a guided tour of the island this morning, followed by a treasure hunt this afternoon."

"Yes, that's fine. I'll sort it all out," Lyle said.

"With prizes," Miss Platt added firmly.

"Don't worry. I'll find some prizes."

Miss Platt pulled her ponytail a little tighter. "All right," she conceded. "That will be fine."

I finished a mouthful of toast and put my hand up. "Yes, Emily?"

"Do we know when Shiprock will get here?" I asked. Mrs. Sharktail wouldn't let them miss their Saturday classes, so they were coming today. Shona had said that they'd be getting marine transportation for most of the way and swimming the last part. I wanted to go and meet them when they arrived.

"I believe they'll be here late afternoon or early evening," Lyle replied. "After I left you last night, I went home and dug out most of the paperwork relating to your week. Hopefully, the rest of it will be as smooth as a freshly washed pebble." He tried to smile. The edges of his mouth went up a tiny smidgen. He looked quite nice when he smiled. Nice, but not happy. The smile definitely didn't get anywhere near his eyes.

"Will you be able to give us our Island Intros and Official Orientation as promised?" Miss Platt asked him.

Lyle nodded. "Yes, of course."

"All right, then. Children, go and get ready and meet me back here in fifteen minutes. Let's get this field trip started, OK?"

As I brushed my teeth, dragged a comb through my hair, grabbed my shoes and coat, and hurried back downstairs, I couldn't help wondering what was in store for us here.

If the rest of the island was as mysterious and odd as Lyle, one thing was for sure: there was no *way* this was going to be your usual boring-as-butterless-bread geography field trip.

Chapter Three

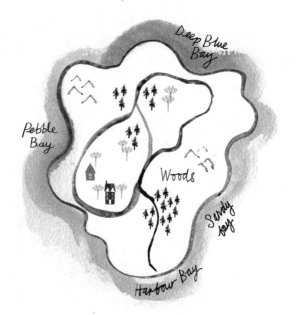

*A*ll right eighth-graders, settle down and face this way, please." We gathered around to listen to Miss Platt.

"Good. Now, can you all get into pairs and take a clipboard and a pencil, one per pair. I'll hand these out. Lyle is passing around some papers. You'll need one of these per pair as well."

I glanced at Mandy.

"It's fine. You go with Aaron," she said. "I'll pair up with Julie."

Aaron smiled as he took a clipboard and came over to me.

Miss Platt was peering into her bag. "I've brought these, too," she said as she pulled out some bright-red rolled-up bags. "Obviously, we are on an island, and I'm sure you'll be tempted to go swimming at some point. If you want to, please put your papers and any valuables into these dry bags to keep them from getting damp and ruined."

I took a dry bag from Miss Platt and shoved it in my jacket pocket.

"Now that you've got everything you need," she went on, "let's listen to Lyle for further instructions."

Miss Platt stepped back as Lyle cleared his throat. "Right. Um. OK. Well, as I've said, it's normally my wife who does this sort of thing, so bear with me." He held up one of the papers. "Each pair should have one of these. You'll see there's a list of questions on the front."

We looked down at the sheet of paper. At the top it said, "Island Intro—Treasure Hunt!" Below the heading there were numbered questions with space between each one for our answers.

"If you turn your papers over, you'll see a map of the island."

I flipped our sheet over and studied the map. There was a rough outline of an island, with straggly lines to mark the paths, groups of contours wiggling around in bendy lines to indicate the hills, some pictures of trees and houses, and the bays with their names in swirly writing.

"Your map indicates the main layout of the island," Lyle explained. "You'll see north is at the top of the island, south at the bottom. There are lines showing all the main paths. It is very important that you stick to these. If it's not on the map, it's possibly dangerous and unstable, so avoid any paths that aren't clear and labeled. The rest should be self-explanatory."

I studied the map a bit more. On the south side of the island, it showed the bay where we'd arrived. This was labeled "Harbor Bay." The map showed a line running from the beach, through some trees, and out to a thicker line with the houses on it. That was the path we'd followed last night. "Sandy Bay," "Deep Blue Bay," and "Pebble Bay" were the only other labels.

I put my hand up.

Miss Platt noticed me. "Yes, Emily?"

"How come it's called Fivebays Island but there are only four bays?"

Miss Platt turned to Lyle. Lyle stared at her without replying. I guess he felt silly for being in charge of an island that had obviously been given the wrong name. "There *are* five bays," he said eventually. "But only four of them are used. Access to the fifth bay is extremely dangerous and not to be attempted. Any other questions?"

No one asked anything else.

"Good. Well. This is a lovely idea." Miss Platt turned to Lyle. "A great way of educating the children about the island as well as getting them to use their initiative. If there are no further questions, let's get going."

Lyle stopped us. "Oh, one last thing. Please bear in mind that there's a big tidal range here. It's low tide in a couple of hours, when the beaches will be at their biggest and all the paths will be accessible. Later on today, you'll need to be careful around the coast as the tide comes in quite high and most of the bays virtually disappear—apart from Sandy Bay. There's always at least a bit of beach there."

Miss Platt looked at Lyle to see if he'd finished. He gave her a quick nod. "Good," she said with a smile. She looked at her watch. "Shall we say, meet back here in two hours?"

"What do the winners get?" Adrian, one of the boys, asked. "You said there were prizes."

Miss Platt turned to Lyle.

"I . . . er . . ." he said. "I forgot about that. I'm sorry."

Miss Platt tutted and frowned. "OK, how about this, then? First pair back—with all the right answers—is the first to be excused from cleanup duties."

"We have to clean up?" Adrian whined.

Miss Platt looked from side to side and behind

her. "Do you see any servants around here?" she asked, with that special brand of sarcasm that only teachers seem to have.

"And, um, cook, too," Lyle added.

"What?" Adrian whined. I have to say, I think most of the class was with him on this one.

Miss Platt tapped her watch. "You'd better get going, then," she said. "If you don't like cooking or cleaning, that is."

The rest of the class hurried off, looking down at their papers. They were heading in the direction of the woods—the way we'd come last night.

I read the first question out loud as we followed the others. "'Go to Harbor Bay and see what's afloat. What's the color of the boat?'"

"That little rowboat by the shed! You and I walked straight past it when we went down to the water's edge," Aaron said. "It was blue. I'm sure. At least, I think I am."

I laughed. "I'd have said the same. I'm almost positive it's blue."

"It *was* pretty dark," Aaron went on. "What do you think? You want to follow all the others down there, or take a chance on blue and get ahead of the game?"

I knew Aaron had a competitive side. I'd seen it when we raced each other in the sea or played chess. And when it was me and him together against everyone else, I wanted to win as much as he did. I liked the idea of being the best team. "Let's go with blue and get ahead," I agreed.

As the rest of the class disappeared into the woods, Aaron looked over my shoulder and read out question number two. "'Sandy Bay is soft and fair, but how many stairs will take you there?'"

I studied the map. "Look, there's Sandy Bay." I pointed at the large bay on the east of the island. "We need to take the path after the woods and it'll lead us to the steps, from the look of it."

Aaron checked behind us to make sure we were the only ones heading straight for the second question, then took my hand. "Come on," he said, half walking, half running. "Let's go."

"One hundred sixty-one, one hundred sixty-two." I looked up and saw that Aaron was way ahead of me.

"Two hundred and seven!" he yelled as he reached the bottom. He scribbled the answer on the sheet.

I stopped where I was. "Does that mean I don't have to bother with the last fifty steps?" I called back.

Aaron waved me down. "You'll regret it if you don't. It's stunning!"

"But that's even more steps to go back up again!"

"Believe me, it's worth it. Come on."

My knees wobbling, I made it to the bottom and looked around. Stretching as far as I could see was a wide pale-yellow sandy beach. In front of us, a thin white line marked the point where the sea lapped against the shore.

Aaron sat on the sand and put the clipboard down. I picked it up and glanced at the next question: *Just how deep is our deepest bay? And please log height and time of day.*

"What are you doing?" I asked as he pulled his sandals off.

"Going for a swim. Come on!"

"What about the treasure hunt? Don't you want to win?"

"Yeah, I guess," he said. "But look at it." He nodded at the sea. Clear turquoise water glinted and winked with a thousand tiny sparkles as the morning sun beamed across it. Farther out, the turquoise gave way to a deeper blue. I could almost hear the waves whispering my name.

"There's still no sign of anyone else yet," Aaron went on. "Let's at least have a quick dip."

I sat next to him and pulled my sandals off too. "OK. Just a quick one, though," I agreed. We rolled up our pant legs and stood up. I grabbed the treasure-hunt sheet and pulled it off the clipboard.

"What are you taking that for?" Aaron asked.

"Just to make sure nothing happens to it while we're gone."

"Good idea. We don't want one of the other teams swiping it and setting us back."

I laughed. "I actually meant it might blow away, but, that's a good point, too."

I folded the sheet, unhooked the pencil, zipped them both into the dry bag we'd been given, and shoved it in my pocket.

"Ready?" Aaron grinned.

"Yep, let's go."

We ran together down to the water's edge. The sand was soft and warm. As we stood ankle-deep in the cool water and Aaron smiled at me, I was pretty sure I'd never felt so happy in my life.

A whole week of this stretched ahead. I was pretty sure I was the luckiest half girl, half mermaid in the whole wide world.

Aaron was looking out to sea. "Em, shall we . . . ?"

I knew what he was asking. Aaron was just like me. To a semi-mer, standing ankle-deep in water is a bit like a chocoholic looking at a shop full of Hershey's bars.

I followed his gaze. The sea was sparkling as if it were covered in jewelry. It seemed to be speaking to us, beckoning us. I couldn't resist. My ankles were already beginning to tingle, and I could feel my toes starting to web together.

"Let's," I said. "It's a beautiful morning. We could have a quick swim, and I'm sure we'll be dry by the time we get to the next question."

"And we'll probably still be ahead of the game." Aaron had already let go of my hand and was wading into the water. He was up to his knees and his pants were wet when he turned around and smiled. "Here goes!" Then he dived right under the water and disappeared.

I had a quick look behind us. There was still no one on the beach. I took a few more steps, then dived in.

The water was smooth and silky and took all my thoughts away as it enveloped me, filling me with warmth. A moment later, I felt my body start to change. My legs tingled and tightened and stretched out. A moment later, they had disappeared altogether.

In their place, my tail had formed. Purple and green, sparkling and bright, it glinted as I flicked it, scattering rainbow droplets of water around me.

We swished along together, through water that was so clear you could see everything. Golden sand lined the seabed. It puffed up into dusty bubbles as we swam over it. Every now and then, we passed a small cluster of rocks with thin strands of seaweed reaching upward like a bouquet of flowers, or a single fish darting past as if in a hurry to get to an appointment. Shoals of fish sailed by, in formations as perfect as gymnastic teams.

I could have stayed there all day.

Except, obviously, we couldn't—not unless we

wanted to get into huge trouble with Miss Platt. The thing about her was, she was one of the nicest teachers at Brightport—always friendly and smiley—but firm enough that we generally did what she said. You always wanted one of her smiles, not one of her stern looks.

Which meant we should get back to the treasure hunt. I didn't want us to be the pair who got the stare for arriving back two hours after everyone else.

I tapped Aaron on the arm. "I think we should head back."

He nodded and pointed upward. "Let's check where we are."

We swam up to the surface and looked around. We'd come a long way out in the short time we'd been swimming. That was the thing with being in the water—you lost track of your bearings; a tail was much quicker than legs.

I could still see Sandy Bay, but we'd swum around the coast as well as out to sea, and as I looked back to land, I noticed we'd almost reached the next bay. Ducking back under the water, I could see a ledge ahead of us, where the seabed dropped right down and the water was even more blue and clear.

Aaron pointed ahead. "This must be Deep Blue Bay! Wasn't the next question taking us here?"

"We have to find out the depth of the deepest bay," I replied.

"So, what do you think? I'd say the deepest bay is probably the one with 'Deep' in its name, wouldn't you?"

"I guess so. Should we take a look?"

"Why not? Maybe we can get in another answer before we go back. We'll be *miles* ahead, then!"

We swam into the bay together. As we crossed the sea shelf, the water grew suddenly colder. I shivered and looked down. Below me, the seabed had practically disappeared. I swam lower and lower, but it didn't seem to be getting closer.

Aaron was beside me. "Wow. Bit weird, isn't it?"

I nodded. "Beautiful, too, though. Look." I pointed at a group of about ten fish ahead of us. They were dark blue with a pale, thin yellow stripe running down each side. They seemed to shine and glint as they moved. Silvery balls that looked like fluffy diamonds, but were probably some kind of rare jellyfish, bounced and danced around us.

We swam lower still. Eventually, we came to the bottom. Huge rocks lined the seabed. In between them, fish of all shapes and sizes moved about lazily, as if there were no need to hurry down here. A lobster reached out a claw in a gentle yoga stretch, then drew it back in. Plants softly opened and closed, like large mouths gently yawning. Long, solitary fish zigzagged between the stones like expert skiers gracefully swooping along a slalom course.

From the seabed, we could barely see the surface.

"How are we going to figure out the depth from here?" I asked. "Maybe we should just go back."

"I agree." Aaron started swimming upward, and I followed him.

As we rose, the water grew gradually clearer again. I realized we were heading in toward the island, not back out to sea. Ahead of us, a rocky cliff rose almost vertically out of the water. It looked like a wall.

I turned to Aaron. "Shall we?"

He nodded and we went to take a closer look.

"Hey!" Aaron pointed at something metallic on the wall as we approached from under the water. "A ladder!"

We followed it as we swam upward.

"Look." I pointed at some markings beside the ladder, spaced at regular intervals. The first one I could see said *450 ft*. Swimming higher, I saw that the next said *500 ft*. A little higher, *550 ft*.

"They're measurements!" Aaron exclaimed. "Swim up to the next one."

We swam higher — *600 ft*.

"You're right," I said. "These must mark the height from the bottom of the bay."

"So we just need to get the reading at the water-line and we've answered the third question!" Aaron grinned. "We're still ahead of the pack!"

We swam up to the surface and looked for the closest number. A little way above it, a marking read *750 ft*.

"Seven hundred fifty feet. Bingo!" Aaron grinned.

"Hmm, that reading is a few feet above the surface," I said. "Let's call it seven hundred and forty-two."

"Perfect."

We looked around. The ladder led up to a flat rock just above the surface of the water. The lower part of the rock was orangey red. A little way up, there was a line where the orangey red gave way to gray. I guessed that marked the highest waterline.

"Shall we get out and get dry?" I suggested. "Then we can check the next question and figure out whether to go back to Sandy Bay or just continue on from here."

"Barefoot," Aaron added.

"Oh, yeah. We should have thought about that!"

We pulled ourselves out of the water and sat on the flat rock. As soon as we did, I felt my tail flicker and twitch. Within moments, it had melted back into my legs. My pants were wet, as was my top.

We shook ourselves like damp dogs and squeezed out the edges of our clothes. Luckily for us, it was a warm day; we'd be dry soon.

I took the bag from my pocket and grabbed the pencil and treasure-hunt sheet. I noted down our answer, along with the time. "Want to know the next question?" I asked.

Aaron squeezed closer to look at the sheet with me. "'Bring back a stone from Pebble Bay. And we'll know if you cheated, by the way,'" he read aloud.

"There must be something special about the stones at Pebble Bay," I mused. I turned over the map to see where it was. On the other side of Deep Blue Bay from where we were, the drawing showed a long, winding path that snaked back up to the main road, and from there down to Pebble Bay. I guessed that would be the route everyone else would take. It was the only one shown on the map.

The problem was, the cliff in between this side and that one was a sharp, sheer face. The only way we could reach that path was to go back in the water and swim across the bay. We'd only just started to get dry. For once, I didn't feel like going back in the water. Plus, when I studied the map a bit more closely, I noticed something else.

It wasn't marked as a path in the same way as the others, but there was a very thin dotted line that led from somewhere a little higher than the rocks we were sitting on, around the coast and directly across to Pebble Bay. It looked about half as long as the "proper" way of getting there.

The other option would be to swim around, but between the two bays, the rocks jutted out a long way. The wiggly line definitely looked like the quickest route.

As I studied the map, Aaron stood up and eyed the rocks behind us.

"Are you thinking what I'm thinking?" I asked, standing up to join him.

"I hope so. Look." He pointed up to the right. "See where there's a gap in the trees and bushes over there?"

I craned my neck to follow where he was pointing. "Uh-huh."

"The gap seems to extend across in a line. Maybe it's some kind of disused path. I bet that path is a shortcut to Pebble Bay! Feel like checking it out?"

I was already shoving the sheet and bag back in my pocket and looking for the first foothold. "You bet," I said, grinning at him. "Let's do it."

Chapter Four

We clambered over the rocks, helping each other on the steep, slippery sides and not thinking about the cuts and bruises our legs would be covered in the next morning. From where we'd been looking earlier, we'd slightly misjudged exactly how many boulders we were going to have to scramble over.

As I was climbing over the ninth or tenth rock, I remembered something else we were ignoring, too.

"Aaron," I said. He was ahead of me, stretching across a jagged boulder.

"What?" he called back.

"Do you remember what Lyle said about the paths?"

"What about them?"

"About them being dangerous? About how we were to stick to the clearly labeled ones?"

Aaron stopped and turned around. "Oh. Yeah. Do you want to turn back and swim?"

I glanced back to where we'd come from. The sea seemed miles away. Ahead, the thin, scraggly path was only about four more boulders from us.

I shook my head. "Come on. Let's just get there. We've come this far already. How much more difficult can it be once we reach the path?"

Which was quite a good question.

Finding the path wasn't the problem. Following it wasn't too difficult, either. I mean, yes, it was a bit overgrown in places, and we had to keep dodging sticky-out branches and avoiding nettles by ducking down or veering sideways or climbing carefully over them one leg at a time. I was beginning to feel like an expert burglar avoiding an elaborate maze of infrared beams. A barefoot burglar, I might add. My feet were going to be raw by the end of the day.

But none of that was the difficult part.

The difficult part was when the path suddenly narrowed to the width of my foot, and one side of it became a sheer drop down the side of a cliff.

My heart thumped hard in my chest—so hard it felt as though it might unbalance me. I stopped walking and gripped a tree branch to steady myself.

"You OK?" Aaron called back.

I didn't dare reply. Even talking felt as if it might knock me off balance. Even breathing.

So I held my breath, carefully studied every footstep, and kept going.

"Em, I said, are you OK?" Aaron twisted around. As he did, I looked up and nodded. Unfortunately, I chose a bad moment to look away from the path, as my next step went right onto something sharp and prickly.

"Youch!" I hopped onto the other foot and slipped on a leaf. A second later, I'd lost my footing altogether. My leg brushed the edge of the path as I fell.

"Aarggghhh!"

Aaron reached back to grab my hand—but he was too late. "Emily!" he yelled.

"Aaron!" I called back as I watched him lose his balance, too.

"Nooooo!"

We bumped and bounced and slid and fell down

and down, through thorns, rocks, bushes. My clothes ripped, my skin burned, and my brain filled with questions.

Why hadn't we listened to Lyle? Why didn't I *ever* listen? Why could I *never* resist an adventure?

And what were our odds of surviving a fall from the top of a steep, craggy, dangerous cliff edge?

"Emily?"

I lifted my head to see Aaron a little ahead of me. He was scrambling to his feet and coming over.

I pulled a few twigs out of my hair and carefully got to my feet. "Ouch!"

"Are you OK?" Aaron was beside me. He had a line of mud down one side of his face and a scratch down the other that was turning redder by the second.

I rubbed my leg. "Just twisted my ankle a bit, I think," I said. "It'll be fine. How about you?" I reached out to touch his cheek. "That looks sore."

"It's nothing," Aaron said. "As long as you're OK, I'm fine."

I looked around. We'd landed in some kind of ditch. We were still a long way from the bottom of the cliff.

"Looks like this ditch broke our fall," Aaron said, looking both ways along it. In one direction, a big tree lay right across the ditch.

I nodded in the opposite direction. "Let's head this way and see if it leads to some kind of path," I suggested.

We walked in silence for a bit, probably both too shell-shocked to know what to say. What if there was no way out of here? The ditch was too far from the edge to jump into the sea. And too high. What if there was no path out of it? We'd all left our phones at the house, as there was barely any reception on the island, so we couldn't get in touch with anyone to tell them where we were — not that we'd be able to tell them that anyway, as we had no *idea* where we were.

Why? Why hadn't we just stuck to the paths as we'd been told? Just when things were going so well, why couldn't I for once —?

"Emily!" Aaron broke into my thoughts. I caught up to him. We'd reached the end of the ditch. On our left, the cliff rose sharply. To our right, it plunged down almost as sharply. But ahead of us, the ditch narrowed down into a thin squiggle and led to something that looked like a path.

Aaron squeezed through the narrow ditch and jumped down onto the path.

I followed him down and looked around. Now

that we were out of the ditch, I could see the sea beneath us, dark-blue water turning into frothy white swirls as it hit the rocks below.

We set off along the path and rounded a bend. The path continued, but down to the side, almost hidden by plants that were growing around it, was what looked like a concrete step. "Aaron, look!"

We went over and pulled the plants to the side. It wasn't just a concrete step. It was a whole staircase leading down — but to what?

Aaron looked at me. "Shall we . . . ?"

Maybe they led all the way down to the sea. If so, perhaps we could swim around to the next bay quicker than we'd get there on foot. It was worth a look, at least. Plus, there was something about the steps that made me *want* to follow them. They felt like an invitation. A hidden staircase on the forbidden side of an island. I mean, who could resist that?

I nodded. "Let's at least check them out," I said, kicking myself even as I said it. Two minutes earlier, I'd asked myself why I could never resist anything unknown and mysterious — and here I was seeking out that very thing! Fact was, I *couldn't* resist — and I didn't want to. The possibility of an adventure would always be more appealing than the urge to stay safe. It's just how I was made, I guess.

"OK. If there's nothing down there, we can always come back up and see if this path leads us back to the road," Aaron said.

I grinned. "I hoped you'd say that."

He pulled the plants to the side and led the way.

The concrete stairs twisted down and down, dotted throughout with branches, bushes, plants, and twigs.

Part of me was thinking we had an awfully steep climb back up if the steps didn't lead anywhere. The other part just wanted to know where on earth these steps were taking us, and *who* on earth had built them.

We had nearly reached the bottom of the cliff. A turn to the left. Three steps down. A turn to the right. Five more steps. Turn left. Then . . .

"Whoa!" Aaron stopped in his tracks. I stopped right behind him.

"Wow," I said. "What the . . . ?"

We glanced at each other, then looked back down. Below us, a low wall marked the end of the steps. To the left of the wall, there was a very short, very steep path leading directly down to some kind of plinth. It looked like a concrete stage. It was semicircular and jutted from the cliff, looking straight out to sea.

Below the plinth, the sides dropped off vertically down to the beach. The fifth bay! The one that wasn't labeled on the map!

Even from the very edge, it was still too far to jump into the sea. Maybe if the tide was in, we could have done it, but there was no way we could survive a drop like that. It was at least the height of a house, and who knew what rocks might lurk beneath the surface?

But it was what was on the stage that took my breath away.

A chair. A big, chunky wooden chair, facing out across the ocean to the far horizon.

I looked at Aaron. He looked at me. Then, without saying another word, we scurried down the last bit of the path, jumped onto the concrete plinth, and went to examine the chair.

It was solid and heavy and seemed to be rooted to the concrete — almost as if it were part of it. It was made of thick dark wood, damp and slightly rotting at the base of each leg. Tiny bits of moss were growing up the back, and every slat was nailed together firm and tight.

"What is it?" I asked as we walked around it. "I mean, I know what it is, obviously. It's a chair. But what is it for?"

"And *who* is it for?" Aaron mused. "Look." He pointed at the seat. "It's more worn than the rest of it." He was right. The seat was scuffed and pale.

"Like someone sits in it regularly!"

"Exactly. But who? And it's odd that someone comes here regularly when it's so hard to reach."

"And supposedly out-of-bounds," I added.

Aaron walked around to the front and sat in the chair. "Beautiful, though, isn't it? Makes me feel like a king." He sat on the seat, upright and arms folded. "Like Neptune, or King Canute, or something." He patted the seat and shuffled to the side. "Join me."

I squeezed in next to him. "King Aaron and Queen Emily," I murmured. "What do you think? Figure we could do a better job than Neptune, if we were in charge of the oceans?"

As soon as the words were out of my mouth, I wanted to take them back. I mean, that was more or less like asking him if he wanted to marry me, wasn't it?

Aaron laughed. "I don't know. He does pretty well—when he's not in such a bad mood that he destroys islands or creates violent thunderstorms out at sea."

In other words, "No, thank you" to that idea! And in case I hadn't gotten the message clearly enough, he turned to stare at me with a really weird look on his face.

"What?" I asked, wondering whether I should try to explain that I hadn't actually just proposed to him or if that would make it even worse.

Aaron shook his head. "Nah, nothing," he replied lightly. Then he shifted away from me and stared hard out to sea.

OK, thanks, Aaron. I got the message loud and clear.

We sat looking out at the sea in silence for a minute. Other than the fact that my face was burning from making a fool of myself and I'd quite happily have hidden under a rock for a while, I could have stayed there all day. Aaron and I here together, sharing a view of the most beautiful wide blue sea. It was as if there was no one in the world except us. Nothing at all moved.

And then . . .

"Aaron." I nudged him.

"What?"

I held my arm straight out ahead, toward the horizon. The tide was a long way out, but there was still a lot of sea. It wasn't the water I was pointing at, though. It was what was *on* the water. "That."

Aaron followed where I was pointing. "A tall ship!" He jumped up out of the seat. I joined him at the edge of the plinth and we stared at the ship.

It looked like something out of a film. A long boat, rising up at the front and back, it had three tall masts with what looked like very straggly white sails hanging loosely from each one.

I squinted into the sunlight to stare at it. It was half facing us, half facing toward the edge of the horizon, and gliding across the water so gently that it almost seemed to be hovering above it.

"Is it coming to the island, do you think?" I asked.

"It seems to be," Aaron replied. "Must be a couple of miles away at least, though."

"Maybe it's something that Lyle's planned for us!"

"That would be so cool!" Aaron turned to me and grinned. "Although, from what we've seen of his organizational skills so far, I wouldn't bet on it."

"Agreed."

We watched the ship a bit longer. It was mesmerizing. One moment, the sails looked torn and useless. The next, they filled with wind, billowing like a proud sergeant major sticking out his chest to fill his lungs with air. Each time it did this, the ship edged forward. The next moment, the sails would drop, falling back to their lifeless, ragged shape.

And then something *really* weird happened. A line of mist seemed to grow from behind the ship, starting beyond the horizon and enveloping the boat, as if someone were creeping up behind it to throw a sheet over it and hide it away.

The mist crept closer and lower, until it was covering the ship completely. Moments later, the sun came out from behind the mist and started to burn it away. It glared so brightly I had to close my eyes.

When I opened them again, the sea was flat, the air was still, and the mist had vanished.

And so had the ship.

Chapter Five

*A*aron looked at me. "Where'd it go?"

I stared out at the sea, waiting for the ship to come back into sight. "Maybe it's just dipped behind a wave," I suggested.

"There *are* no waves. The sea is as flat as a flounder," Aaron said. "There's no wind . . ."

"And no ship," I finished.

Aaron shook his head. "Maybe it turned and went back over the horizon while the mist was covering it."

"I guess so. It must have changed course," I said, although, to be honest, I could hardly see how. The ship had been hidden by the mist for only a few seconds, half a minute at the most. But I couldn't think of any other possibilities. That *must* have been what had happened.

Aaron glanced at his watch. "I bet we'll be last in the treasure hunt by now."

I looked across toward the steep steps. "Come on, let's head back anyway. You never know, we might have gotten far enough ahead with the first few questions that we still have a chance."

I pulled the sheet out of my pocket and studied the map. Now that we'd discovered the fifth bay, I could figure out where we were on the island. A tiny squiggly line led from here back to the main road. That would be the one we'd found at the end of the ditch.

I pointed at the map to show Aaron where we were. "We just have to go back up the steps, then take the path up that way, and we should get back on track."

"OK. Let's go. What was the next question again?"

I turned the sheet over and read it out. "'Bring back a stone from Pebble Bay. And we'll know if you cheated, by the way.'"

"OK. Pebble Bay, it is," Aaron said as he headed back across the plinth to the steps. "Let's see if we can get back in the race."

Needless to say, we didn't win the treasure hunt. Luckily, some of the others had found a few places difficult to find, so we didn't come in last, either. We were somewhere around the middle—good enough not to attract attention, despite coming back looking like extras from a street urchin scene in *Oliver Twist*.

We caught up with the rest of the class at the finish point in the woods. Mandy gave me a wave. She and Julie were sitting with some of the others at the foot of a tree farther down the path.

"What happened to you?" Mandy asked me.

"What do you mean?"

She pointed at my left arm. "You've got a massive bruise all down your arm."

I twisted my arm to study it. She was right. It was turning bluish purple already, and there was a cut streaking down the center of the bruise.

"And your other arm is bleeding," Mandy added. "Plus, your legs are covered in mud. And you're limping."

"We got a bit lost," I said casually. Then I added in a whisper, "I'll tell you more later." Miss Platt was coming up behind us, and I didn't want her to overhear me telling Mandy that we'd deliberately set off down a path to a bay that we'd been specif-ically told to keep away from.

"OK. And, um . . . you do know you're not wearing any shoes, don't you?" Mandy added.

I nodded. "I'll explain that later, too."

"All right, kids. Well done, all of you. Let's head back to the house now," Miss Platt said as she gathered us together. "Go and get yourselves cleaned up and we'll meet in the dining room in twenty minutes. After lunch, you can have some free time while Lyle and I mark the treasure-hunt sheets. Please, can I have some volunteers to help prepare the food?"

We shuffled quickly across the road and over to the house before Miss Platt "volunteered" us for kitchen duties.

"Did you see that amazing ship?" I asked Mandy as we went to the room we were sharing with some of the other girls.

"Which ship?" Mandy asked.

"Big tall ship out on the horizon with massive sails. It looked like it was coming this way but changed course."

"Er, nope." Mandy shook her head. "Are you sure you didn't imagine it?" she joked, reminding me it wasn't so long ago that she'd bullied me and taunted me and called me names. Those days were gone now, though, weren't they?

Mandy must have seen me flinch. "Hey, I'm just

53

teasing," she said more gently. "I was probably on the other side of the island when you saw it."

"Yeah, probably," I agreed. But I wasn't too sure—and I decided not to mention the ship again, to Mandy *or* anyone else. Something about it was niggling at me. What was it? The way it had moved? The way it had seemed to come from nowhere and disappear so suddenly? The sails that at one moment had looked ragged and torn and the next had filled with air to propel the ship forward?

Or all of it?

Either way, as I dug in to my chips and my cheese-and-pickle sandwich, I forgot about the ship and got back to the things that really mattered: planning what to do with my friends in our free time.

It wasn't a difficult decision. The sun was still shining, and Mandy and Aaron agreed with me: Sandy Bay was our free time destination.

The first thing we did when we got there was look for our sandals. The tide had come in quite a bit since Aaron and I had been down here earlier, but it was still a long way from the top of the beach. They were exactly where we'd left them.

Mandy took her shoes and socks off and put

them with ours. "Let's go for a wade," she suggested. Then she stopped and looked from Aaron to me. "I mean, if that's . . . if it wouldn't make you . . . if you don't mind . . ."

"It's fine," I assured her. "We don't sprout tails until we're halfway into the water. Even if we did, it's not a problem." I rolled up my pant legs and waved the others on. "Come on, race you!"

We ran down the beach and into the water. Some of our classmates had had the same idea and come down to Sandy Bay, too. We joined them, splashing one another and racing along the shore, shrieking as we ran.

Then Mandy stopped running and pointed out to sea. "Hey, look," she said.

My heart quickened. Was it the ship again? I looked where she was pointing. It wasn't the ship. It was even better than that—a shoal of dolphins was swimming, diving, and zooming through the waves. They were carrying bags on their backs. And there were people in between the dolphins.

Shiprock School had arrived!

I looked at Mandy. She smiled. "It's fine. Go and meet them. There are plenty of others on the beach," she said, reading my mind in a way that she had never done before, and that only really good friends do. I smiled back and couldn't help thinking how far we'd come since the days when she'd called me "fish girl."

Without stopping to think, I gave her a hug. "Thanks, Mandy," I said.

She awkwardly hugged me back, then pulled away. "You're soaking me!"

I laughed. "Like you're not already drenched."

She shrugged. "True." Then she nodded toward the group coming ever closer. "Go on. Go and welcome them to the island."

I dived into the water and swam out to meet them. Aaron had been playing football with some of the other boys on the beach, but when he saw me turn and dive into the water, he swam out to join me.

Shona was right at the front of the group. We practically swam headfirst into each other.

"Emily!" Shona beamed as she pulled me into the biggest hug.

"You're early!" I said as we swam along. "I thought you weren't coming till tonight."

"We were loaned Neptune's top fleet of dolphins, so we made it in half the time."

Aaron whistled. "Nice. How did you manage that?"

At which point, someone else swam up beside Shona. "It helps if you have the right contacts," he said with a grin.

"Seth!" Aaron swam over to Seth and slapped him on the back. "How come you're here?"

"He came up with an ingenious plan," Shona said.

Seth continued, "I persuaded Neptune that something as important as the first joint school outing between merfolk and humans needed someone to supervise it."

Shona smiled at Seth. "Seth made it sound like Neptune's idea."

"And Neptune went for it!" Seth finished with a grin. "So here I am! Probably just for a couple of days, but it's better than nothing."

"Swishy!" I said.

"Isn't it?" Shona added shyly.

"So where are you staying?" I asked Shona.

"Mr. Finsplash says it's close to one of the bays. Dark Blue Bay, is it?"

"Deep Blue Bay?" Aaron suggested.

"That's it. There are some tunnels there that have been adapted into a mer-motel."

"Cool. That's where Aaron and I went earlier," I said. "It's just around this corner."

As we passed the rocks at the far edge of Deep Blue Bay, we swam up to the surface to take in the surroundings. It looked different from this morning. Then, the sea had filled the area of the bay, but it hadn't come up as high.

Now the water came so far up the cliffs, you couldn't see the orangey red of the low rocks. We'd thought it was deep earlier. Now it was probably half as deep again. The water had more energy, too. It lifted and lowered us as we talked.

"It's the deepest bay on the island," Aaron said.

"There are five bays, but we're allowed to visit only four of them." I added.

"Not that we took any notice of—"Aaron began.

He was interrupted by Mr. Finsplash calling everyone back down to follow him.

"We'll catch up with you later, OK?" Shona said. "They've told us we're all meeting up in a bit, at the edge of this bay."

"Great! See you later," I said, and Shona and Seth ducked back down under the water.

Aaron and I were about to do the same and start heading back to Sandy Bay when something caught my eye on the cliffs. Or someone.

"Aaron," I said. "Look." Two of the others from our class were standing on the rocks, near to where we'd been earlier. They were perched on a rocky ledge below the path we'd walked along. They looked as if they were in trouble.

Aaron stared at the cliff. "That's James and Annabel. What are they doing?"

We swam over to them and called up. Now that the tide was nearly high, we weren't that far away from them—close enough to see their faces. They looked terrified. "Are you OK?" I called up.

Annabel just shook her head without replying. James called back to us.

"We're stuck," he said. "We walked around the top of the bay earlier, but we can't get back now. We didn't realize the tide would come in so quickly."

I glanced across the rocks and saw what he meant. The water had risen so high, the two sides of the bay were now cut off from each other. As the tide inched ever higher, the swell was lifting and dropping us. One second, we were calling to them from a long way down; the next we were virtually slammed up against the cliffside.

"Why don't you jump into the water?" I suggested. "Or climb down the ladder? We'll swim across the bay with you."

Annabel violently shook her head. "No way," she called, watching the water crash against the rocks. "I'm not getting in there."

A moment later, the sea itself replied to her fear. A wave rose so high and so violently against the cliff, it was as if it were reaching out to snatch and grab whatever it could for the ocean.

Annabel let out a scream and pressed herself as far against the back of the rocky ledge as she could. Two more waves rose up and lashed at the cliff— each one searching the rocks for debris to steal. The next three were calmer, but still pretty fierce.

I vaguely remembered Annabel's attempts in the

pool, back in Brightport. She was one of the weaker swimmers. I wasn't surprised she was reluctant to take on the biggest, deepest bay, especially when there were waves like this to contend with.

I studied the coastline. She and James weren't too far from where we'd come out of the water that morning. It wouldn't be the easiest thing in the world for us to clamber up the ladder while the swell was this heavy, but I figured if we could get out and join them, we could help them back to the path.

Aaron looked at me. He was thinking the same thing—I could tell. "Let's get out and help them," he said.

I nodded. "Just stay where you are," I called. "We're coming up."

Aaron and I waited for one of the less ferocious waves to raise us up, then we grabbed the ladder and climbed out of the water as fast as we could, before the next wave slammed us against the side. We held on to the top of the ladder as we waited for our tails to fade away and our legs to reform. Then we scrambled across to join Annabel and James.

"Thank you so much!" Annabel cried as we reached them and got our breath back from the climb.

I looked around. "OK, we just need to climb over a few of these rocks, and the path will be ahead of us."

"I thought the path was that way," James said, pointing across the bay.

"This is a different path," Aaron explained. "You don't know it's there till you get over these rocks. Come on, follow us."

Aaron and I took the lead. We clambered over the boulders like expert rock climbers this time. The final one was the toughest, and I reached down to grab Annabel's hand and help her. Once we were all past the rock, the path opened up ahead of us. Aaron set off along it, and we followed behind him in single file.

"The path gets really narrow in a bit," I said over my shoulder as we walked. "Just stay calm and keep putting one foot in front of the other. You'll be fine."

We walked on silently till we came to the point where we'd fallen earlier.

"Careful here," Aaron called back.

A few minutes later, we reached the path that led down to the chair. Part of me wanted to go back down there to see it again. The other part wanted to keep it a secret, just for Aaron and me. I couldn't resist a glance as we passed, though.

I could see the steep drop down the cliff and the very edge of the plinth. From here, the chair was just out of sight.

"OK, we take this path here," Aaron said, waiting for the others to catch up. Their faces were white from their cliff-edge walk. "It's inland from here, and a much safer path all the way back to the road."

"Thank you so much for doing this," Annabel said as she started up the path. I was waiting at the corner for them to come past me. "I don't know what we'd have done if you hadn't been there."

"I don't even want to think about it," James added.

I didn't want to think about it, either. With the tide rising and the waves hitting the cliffside like they were, I guessed that another few minutes on that rock and the two of them would have been in serious trouble.

The others had gone ahead of me up the path. I was about to follow them when I heard something below us. It sounded like a splash. I glanced in the direction of the plinth, just in time to see a widening circle of ripples, spreading and growing like when you throw a stone into a lake—only much bigger and wider.

Then I saw something even more peculiar—below the surface of the water, a dark shadow was moving away from the ripples. What was it? A shark? A big fish? And what had caused the splash?

"Emily, are you coming?" Aaron called. The three of them had stopped to wait for me. Should I tell them what I'd seen? I looked back down. The shape under the water had disappeared now; the ripples had almost gone. What was there to tell? It was just a fish. And the ripples must have been caused by a loose piece of rock falling from the cliff. I mean, what other explanation was there?

"Coming," I replied, and headed up the path to join my friends, trying to put my questions about this strange corner of the island to the back of my mind.

Chapter Six

We rejoined the road at the top of the path and found our way back to the house.

"There you are," Miss Platt said, greeting us at the door. "We're meeting out here in five minutes. Shiprock School has arrived, and we're all going to Deep Blue Bay to discuss plans for the week. Hurry, hurry. Don't make us late."

I ran upstairs, quickly got changed, and joined the others a few minutes later. As we walked, I told Aaron about what I'd seen earlier. "I'm sure it was a big fish or a shark or something," I said. "Just, it looked . . . well, like a person."

"It was probably one of the kids from Shiprock," Aaron said.

Of course! Why hadn't I thought of that?

"What about the ripples, though?"

Aaron shrugged. "Whoever it was must have flip-dived into the water or something." He laughed.

"What?"

"Just you. You're determined to find mystery and adventure everywhere you go, aren't you?"

I shrugged and folded my arms. "No," I said defensively.

Aaron laughed again and slipped an arm around my waist. "No need to sulk," he said. "I meant it as a compliment. It's one of the things I—"

He stopped and coughed. "Sorry, swallowed a fly," he said, thumping his chest a couple of times.

"One of the things . . ." I prompted him when he'd gotten over his coughing fit.

"Just, you know, it's why I don't mind hanging out with you," he said lightly.

He doesn't mind hanging out with me? Was that all he thought of me? When I'd been practically picturing us getting married! That put *me* in my place!

"Come on, we're getting behind." And with that, he sped up and practically marched to the front of the group.

"Now, then, children. Please remember we are not only making history this week; we are also here to learn about each other's worlds," Miss Platt began. We were huddled at one end of the bay, sitting on the ground, leaning against the boulders that lined the shore. It was the only bit of land that we could sit on. The rest was cut off by the tide now. The Shiprock class was in the sea in front of us.

Mr. Finsplash rose a little higher in the water. "Well said, Miss Platt," he agreed.

"Please, call me Andrea," Miss Platt said with a tiny blush.

Mr. Finsplash smiled at Miss Platt. "Very well. In that case, you must call me Kal."

Miss Platt returned the smile. "Thank you, Kal. I shall."

Mandy nudged me and winked. I laughed.

Miss Platt shot us a warning look as Mr. Finsplash continued. "I am in full agreement with Miss . . . with Andrea. We are here to learn, to share, and to enjoy everything that this splendid island has to offer." He glanced around. "Now, I believe that a Lowenna Waters is going to tell us what we are doing next."

Miss Platt stepped forward. "Actually, Lowenna

66

isn't here. She's . . . well, actually, we don't know exactly what's happened to her, but we believe she's been called away. Her husband, Lyle, is taking care of us."

"Fine. Let's hand it over to Lyle, then," Mr. Finsplash said, looking around again, presumably wondering which one of the children in front of him might possibly be a man named Lyle, who was married to Lowenna and in charge of today's activities.

"Lyle isn't here," Miss Platt said tightly. "We looked for him at his house on the way here, but he—"

"Miss Platt, look!" One of the girls, Evie, was pointing to the other side of the bay, where Lyle was hurrying across to join us.

"I'm so sorry to keep you waiting," he said breathlessly as he rushed over. He looked as if he'd just gotten out of the shower.

Smoothing down his wet hair and half tucking his shirt into his pants, Lyle gave Mr. Finsplash and the Shiprock kids an awkward wave. "I'm Lyle," he said. "Welcome to Fivebays Island."

Mr. Finsplash raised a disapproving eyebrow. "Nice to meet you," he said stiffly.

"All right, then. We're all here now," Miss Platt said. "Shall we get on with the activity, then?"

"The . . . ah, yes," Lyle said.

"You *do* have an activity for us?" Miss Platt asked impatiently.

"Um. Well, actually, I . . ."

Miss Platt shot a *This-is-what-we've-had-to-put-up-with* look at Mr. Finsplash, who decided to jump in and save the day — probably to impress *Andrea*.

"I've got an idea," he said brightly. "First, let's split into boys and girls." We all dutifully shuffled into position in our separate groups.

"Now, all of you form pairs."

We started shuffling again. I looked for Mandy to see if she wanted to pair up with me.

"I hadn't finished," Mr. Finsplash announced. We stopped shuffling. "One human, one mer in each pair."

That was easy. I sought out Shona in the group in the water. She gave me a nod and a thumbs-up.

Miss Platt clapped her hands together like she does when one of us comes up with a good answer. "Wonderful idea!" she trilled. Taking over from Mr. Finsplash, she went on. "In your pairs, we'd like each of you to teach the other something new about your worlds."

"And about the island," Lyle interjected, glancing at both teachers as if they were in charge and he was the overeager student.

"And about the island," Miss Platt agreed.

"You'll have to figure out how to do this together," Mr. Finsplash added. "Deal with the limitations you have in exploring each other's worlds, and together find a way to overcome any obstacles."

Lyle looked at his watch. "It's high tide in an hour. How about we meet at Sandy Bay just after that? There won't be much space here for the Brightport students when the tide is fully in."

"Perfect," Miss Platt agreed.

"In your pairs, we want you to tell us what you have learned about each other's worlds, and then tell us something you have discovered together about the island," Mr. Finsplash concluded. "Any questions?"

Tommy put his hand up. "Yeah. Miss Platt, are you and Mr. Finsplash going to teach each other about your worlds, too?"

We all started to laugh, till a look from Miss Platt stopped us. Her eyes were stern, but her pink cheeks gave her away.

"Yes, Tommy," Mr. Finsplash said. "That's a very good idea. OK. What are you waiting for? Team up and get going. We'll see you in just over an hour at Sandy Bay."

With that, the two groups shuffled and jostled and awkwardly made introductions. Luckily for Shona and me, our teachers were too interested in getting to know each other to worry about whether it was cheating if we teamed up when we were already best friends.

I slid into the water, and Shona and I swam off to gossip, chat, and catch up while the others discussed how to go about their assignment.

We got right down to important matters.

"So, are you and Seth officially boyfriend and girlfriend yet?" I asked Shona as we swam off. We stayed above the surface of the water, gently flicking our tails as we meandered out to sea.

"I don't know," she admitted. "He hasn't mentioned it and neither have I. Maybe we'll figure it out while we're here. You like him, don't you?"

"Hmmm. A good-looking boy who saved the narwhal from certain death, is one of Neptune's closest advisers, and clearly adores you . . . Let me think!" I teased.

"You think he's good-looking?"

"Of course. Obviously not as good-looking as Aaron, but, you know, he's OK."

Shona laughed and splashed water at me. "Come on, let's explore," she said, diving under the surface. I followed her down.

I marveled, as I always did, at the change in life under the water. I'd been a mermaid for only the last year. Or, at least, I'd only *known* I was a mermaid for that long, so it was all still relatively new to me — the silence of the underwater world, the bright colors, the gentle swaying of the plant life at the bottom of the ocean.

We zigzagged through a mini forest of seaweed. Bright-green tubes with feathery yellow tops, reaching up toward the surface of the sea, jostled against one another and stretched upward, like a crowd of people all craving a glimpse of the sky.

We raced alongside a pair of sleek black fish. They looked like mini skinny sharks: focused and serious. Long-tailed, long-nosed, and fast, they seemed to be on a mission. They barely flicked their tails as they sped through the water. We let them zoom ahead.

We swam past a shoal of tiny black fish, swimming around and around to a spinning circle, constantly on the move, like a snowball getting bigger and bigger as it rolls down a hill.

Below us, the sandy seabed was broken up by occasional clumps of rocks and weeds. In among them, crabs and lobsters lay in wait, like old men sitting outside their houses watching the world go by and meeting up for games of chess and dominoes.

"Hey, look," I said, pointing ahead. The clumps of rocks seemed to give way to something else. Or, rather, they seemed to *build* into something else. The individual clusters of rock became bigger and bigger, until there was no sand at all. Just rocks. The water grew colder as we swam above them.

"Look over there," Shona said, gesturing ahead to where the rocks grew even higher and darker.

We swam carefully toward them, weaving

between the jagged tops that reached higher and higher. Some of the peaks almost came to the surface of the water.

"It's like a mountain range," I whispered.

"It's incredible," Shona agreed.

As we swam over a particularly high peak, my tail brushed against the rock. It almost scratched me; it was cold, rough. I was about to suggest we forget it and turn back when I noticed something.

"Shona, it's like a secret path!" On the other side of the peak, the range fell steeply away. It was a sheer drop down, not just from this peak but all the way along the rocks. Suddenly, the seabed was a long, long way down. The water was clear, blue, warm. I could see the sandy surface way down below us, a thin winding channel within the rocky mountain range.

Shona and I stared along the channel, then turned to gape at each other.

"OK, I have officially *never* seen anything like this," Shona admitted.

"You want to explore?"

Shona twisted uncomfortably. As she did, her tail glinted and sparkled in the newly clear water. "I don't know if we should," she began. "I mean, we've been out for quite a while. Maybe we should start heading back."

I'd dragged Shona into a lot of adventures in the past, and some of them had been pretty life-threatening. I wasn't going to draw her into another one if she wasn't up for it. I started to turn around to swim back. "OK, you're right," I said. "We probably should be heading—"

"No." Shona stopped me. I don't know if she'd seen the disappointment on my face or if something about this hidden channel had ignited her curiosity, too, but she pulled me back. "Come on. We might never find it again. Let's just have a quick look. I'm sure we've got time."

So we swam on. The channel narrowed and twisted and turned, like a giant eel snaking along the ocean floor. We followed each curve and bend, marveling at the huge sheer cliff faces on either side of us as we swam.

We passed shoals of tiny white-and-yellow fish, swimming along in a line like an obedient brood of ducklings behind their mother, and shoals of blue-and-purple striped fish, wide and round, moving along in perfect formation like a dance troupe.

Three sleek black fish darted through the channel beside us before racing ahead, like commuters hurrying to their offices. Small nests of seaweed bunched up here and there, green strands with their feathery yellow tops waving us on through the channel as tiny sand clouds puffed up between them.

And then something weird happened. . . .

Everything stopped.

The fish scattered and disappeared around the

next bend. The seabed no longer sent up puffs of sand. Even the rocks seemed more still. All the motion of the ocean had frozen.

And then . . .

I gulped as I stared ahead—too shocked to speak, too enthralled to turn back and grab Shona. Coming around the bend and heading directly toward us was the huge, dark hull of a ship.

I tried to turn and swim away, but my tail had forgotten how to work. I couldn't move. The ship was coming right at me—an enormous deep-blue hull with some kind of gold figurehead rising up out of the water at the bow. Any second now, it would hit me. What could I do? There was nowhere to escape to, no room in this channel to dive out of its way. I could dive down to the bottom, but to be honest, I didn't really like the idea of a massive ship gliding directly over me. Which just left one other option: head upward.

Without pausing for another moment, I spun my tail as hard as I could and propelled myself upward. If I could get to the surface and out onto the top of the rocky peaks, perhaps I could get out of the ship's way—everyone knows ships avoid rocks!

Panting and gasping, I reached the surface and looked around. The ocean was as calm and still as the channel below. The surface of the sea lay like a blue-tinted mirror: shiny, flat, glass-like. It was eerie. But that wasn't the strangest thing.

The strangest thing was the sight ahead of me—the ship. It was the only thing around that showed any sign of movement. Its sails were billowing and then dropping, as if begging for wind—searching for the tiniest bit of breath in the air to propel the ship forward. But there was nothing, no wind to give it power.

Aside from its flapping sails, the ship was as still as everything else. Out there in the wide, open sea, it appeared to sit firm on the ocean, motionless.

I swam around its sides, looking at it from every angle. The hull was dark blue, with a white line that ran all the way around. The sides fanned out and upward, with the longest bowsprit I'd ever laid eyes on—that's the big wooden pole that sticks out from the front of the ship. I'd never seen one like it. Beneath the pole, an intricate maze of ropes formed a netted hammock. Three huge masts stretched upward from the deck, sails now flapping uselessly.

I'd seen these sails and this ship before, from the chair on the edge of the cliff. Surely it couldn't be . . .

I wasn't a hundred percent certain, but it was so similar, and you didn't often see tall ships like this. It *had* to be the same one.

Up close, I could see the figurehead below the bowsprit. The top was a woman's face and torso with long hair stretching the length of her body. Her bottom half was a tail. I would have said the figurehead was a mermaid, except that the tip of her tail opened out into a jagged-edged fan, with swirling patterns and fire snaking along the hull below it. Part mermaid, part dragon? Freaky, whatever it was.

I swam alongside the hull. There were letters at the bow. I read them as I swam by: *Prosperous II,* the ship's name.

I swam toward the stern — that's the back end of the ship. Swimming away from the ship so I could see higher, I craned my neck and looked up. A wide, flat wooden deck looked polished to perfection. From the water, I could see only the edges of it, but it looked almost brand-new.

And then, as I scanned my eyes across the planks, they seemed to come to life! Either I was seeing some sort of weird optical illusion from the sunlight that was shining on the water and sending sparkles across the deck or there was some kind of disco going on up there!

And there was something else — people. A man was sitting on a bench near the stern. A woman was twirling around the edges of the dance floor. Another group of people stood by the rails, looking through binoculars and pointing out to sea.

Who *were* these people? Where had they come from? And why were they so silent?

"Hey!" I yelled. No one responded. No one even turned around. Maybe they were too busy having fun.

I looked around. Where was Shona? What the heck was going on here?

An unpleasant cold feeling snaked through my body from my head to the tip of my tail. I suddenly felt too alone out here, with this.

I dived back under the water and back down into the channel.

"Shona!" I called. Nothing. Where was she?

The hull of the ship was still there, still dark, still huge. I swam toward it. "Shona?" I called again, less certainly.

I moved on, alongside the ship, heading back toward the bow and to where I'd last seen Shona. A line of large portholes was dotted all the way along the hull. As I passed them, I glanced inside. Each one looked into a tiny cabin. They were all empty.

Until I came to one about halfway along.

I swam toward it and glanced in, expecting to see the same dark emptiness inside. What I saw this time made me leap back so hard I hit my head against a rock.

A woman. As I peeked in, she hurried to the porthole and started banging her hand against the glass. Her hair was long and red, straggly and messy. Her eyes were green and wide open. Her fists pumped against the window. Who was she? Was she real? A ghost? A mermaid? *What?*

The woman banged harder against the glass. Her fists didn't make any sound at all—but the urgency of her movements was matched by the expression on her face. She needed help. What could I do?

Her lips were desperately mouthing something, but I couldn't make out the words clearly. It looked like she was saying, "All my weather" or "I'm a winner." What could it mean?

I shook my head as I stared. "I don't know what you're saying!" I shouted to her.

She called something back that looked like "Happy! Happy!" But surely she couldn't be saying that! The very last thing she looked was happy.

She continued repeating the same thing—her mouth forming the words more and more urgently each time. And then I realized what she was saying over and over again. It wasn't "Happy! Happy!"

It was "Help us! Help us!"

I stared at the woman, powerless and panicked. How could I help them? Who were they? Where had they come from?

All I had were questions. I stared back at her, my own face reflected in the glass of the porthole beside hers. I looked almost as panicked as she did.

As I watched, something started to change. The water was moving again. Something was brushing past me. Feathery, long hair covering my face, getting in my eyes. I pulled it away, but it kept on coming. Then it was on my body, my tail. An arm grabbed me around my waist, pulling me down, snatching me away. Cold fingers stabbed me in the side.

No! Please, no!

I shut my eyes and screamed.

The hands were still on me. Grabbing my elbow, shaking me.

"Emily!"

I kept my eyes closed as tightly as I could. I wasn't going to look. I didn't want to see it. A sea monster, a servant of Neptune's sent to kidnap me. I'd been through that before. I couldn't face it happening again.

"Emily!"

Wait. I knew that voice. I opened my eyes. When I did, I saw three things. They registered slowly, one by one, as my brain took each of them in.

Thing one: The person who had called my name was Shona.

Thing two: The hands and monsters grabbing at me were in fact long trails of seaweed that I'd somehow gotten caught up in.

Thing three: The enormous, mysterious, non-moving ship—that a moment ago had practically filled the entire valley—was gone.

Chapter Seven

"What . . . ? Where . . . ? Where is it?" I stammered.

"Where's what?" Shona replied. "Em, are you OK?"

I looked at her. "Am I OK?" I echoed numbly.

"You're shaking."

I held out an arm. Shona was right. My hand was wobbling like a jellyfish. "I . . . The ship," I said. "Where'd it go?"

Shona stared at me. "What ship?"

I laughed. Out of nerves, maybe. "The huge, great, massive ship that was right here!"

Shona shook her head. "Em, I honestly don't know what you're talking about. I've been here the whole time and there hasn't been any ship in sight, I can tell you."

I took a second, tried to calm myself down.

"In fact, I was actually going to ask what had happened to you," Shona went on.

"What do you mean?"

"Just, well, you were acting a bit funny."

"Funny?"

Shona shrugged. "Yeah, like, you were here but kind of weren't at the same time. You were swimming along as though you were looking at something," she said. "You darted up to the surface, so I followed you. I was behind you, but you were facing away from me the whole time, just staring. I called you, but it was like you didn't even hear me."

"You followed me up?"

"Yes, and I—"

"Then you *must* have seen the ship!" I insisted. I jabbed my finger at the empty space in front of us. "It was right *there*! The only thing you could see for miles around—an enormous thing with three masts and ragged sails and . . ."

I stopped. Shona was looking at me with an expression on her face that seemed to say, *I really think this person could do with some help, but I'm not professionally qualified to provide it.*

I stopped trying to explain. What was the point? "You didn't see the ship," I said flatly.

"There *was* no ship," Shona insisted.

I nodded. Resigned to the weirdness. I mean, it had to happen at some point, didn't it? After everything I'd been through in the last year, it was only ever going to be a matter of time before I started losing it completely.

Then Shona said, more gently, "At least, *I* didn't see a ship. But maybe I missed it. I guess I could have been looking the other way."

I laughed. It wasn't exactly the kind of thing you could have missed. "Look," I said. "Just tell me this. You're my best friend, right?"

"Of course I am."

"And you trust me?"

"With my life."

"So, OK, I know it doesn't make sense, but believe me, please. There was a ship. It was right here. I saw it with my own eyes. I *know* it doesn't make sense, and I have no idea how come you didn't see it, but I *swear* that I did."

Shona held my gaze for a moment. "I believe you," she said. "You're right; it *doesn't* make sense; it isn't really possible. But I know you wouldn't make something like that up. You never have before, and I can tell you've seen something weird by how shaky you are. I promise I didn't see anything, but I *do* believe that you did."

I smiled a wobbly smile at her. "Thank you," I said. OK, so I might be completely cracking up, but at least I had Shona to catch the pieces.

And then I realized who else I had: Aaron! He saw the ship, too. At least . . . he did see it, didn't he? He hadn't just pretended to see it to keep me happy? I had to know.

I started swimming back the way we'd come. "Let's get to Sandy Bay," I said. "We'll be the last ones there at this rate."

As we swam, one thought propelled me forward: *Aaron is the only one who can tell me I'm not going completely crazy.*

"Well done, children. You've all done a great job." Miss Platt was sitting on the sand at the water's edge, smiling around at us. I wondered if her super-bright smile had anything to do with her special *getting-to-know-you* time with Mr. Finsplash.

The Brightport kids were sitting on the sand, too. The Shiprock merchildren were mostly lying in the shallows at the water's edge, leaning on their elbows and flapping their tails in the waves.

I'd gotten out of the water when we'd arrived, and

my tail had fizzled away as my legs had reappeared. Now I sat nervously on the sand, my toes on the edge of the soft waves that brushed my feet.

"Who'd like to tell us about what they learned on this assignment?" Miss Platt asked.

One of the Shiprock girls put her hand up.

Mr. Finsplash nodded at her. "Thank you, Izela. Who did you pair up with?"

"Brooke," she replied.

"Excellent. Why don't you both start us off?" Miss Platt said with a smile. "Tell us what you learned about each other's worlds and about Fivebays Island."

I half listened as each pair recounted what they'd learned. And I smiled gratefully when it was our turn and Shona piped up with how we'd discovered a variety of seaweed that she had never encountered before.

But I was only half there. The other half of me couldn't stop thinking about the ship. Aaron was sitting beside me. As we'd expected, Shona and I had been the last pair back, so I hadn't had a chance to talk to him yet. Mandy was sitting on my other side.

"Well, we're very pleased with your first joint assignment. I think it's going to be a swishy week," Mr. Finsplash said when all the pairs had reported back. "Now, it's getting late, so we'll break for dinner. But just before that, Mr. Waters is going to tell you a bit about what we'll be doing tomorrow."

Lyle cleared his throat. "Do call me Lyle," he said.

Mr. Finsplash gave him a curt nod. "Lyle, then," he said awkwardly. "Listen up, all of you, and Lyle will tell us what's in store for us next."

Lyle pulled a piece of paper out of his pocket and unfolded it. "So, tomorrow's task . . . Let's see, now . . . Tomorrow is Monday . . ." he muttered as he looked down at the page.

"Great," Mandy muttered. "He hasn't even bothered to prepare."

"Ah. Here we are. OK. Tomorrow is . . ." Lyle stopped, cleared his throat, glanced up at us all, and opened his mouth like a fish silently trying to get oxygen.

His face had turned gray. He swallowed hard before looking back down at the piece of paper.

"What is his *problem*?" Mandy whispered in my ear.

I shrugged. "I have no idea. Maybe he can't read," I whispered back.

"Or maybe he needs glasses," Mandy offered.

Lyle was talking again. "Sorry," he said. "As I was saying, tomorrow's activity is . . ." He paused again. "It's . . . um . . . It's called Shallows and Shipwrecks."

Something cold grabbed my middle.

"The, um, the island is, as you know, surrounded by reefs and rocks and is in one of the most beautiful and varied parts of the ocean," Lyle went on. His voice sounded mechanical, a bit like a recording made by a machine rather than an actual person talking. It was flat, toneless. "That is why it is so rife with the sea life we have here, and why the island is such a rich source of knowledge and research."

Lyle paused again. He wiped his forehead. He was sweating. What was up with him? Maybe he was sick.

"But there is another side to this," he went on, "which is that the island is also in one of the most *hazardous* parts of the ocean. Only the very skillful and the very experienced can navigate these waters."

Lyle paused—for dramatic effect? Then, in a quieter voice, so quiet we found ourselves leaning forward to hear him, he added, "And that is why we have more shipwrecks in this area than in almost any other stretch of water in all of the oceans."

Something seemed to change when he said this. Was it just me or did the air feel a bit stiller, a bit thinner, a bit less easy to breathe?

His words were dancing around in my brain, teasing my thoughts. Was it a shipwreck that I'd seen? Was that what it was?

Lyle was still talking. "So, tomorrow, you will be studying some of these wrecks. The Shiprock team will be given a map that will take them on a trail of the shipwrecks themselves. The Brightport group will join me in the Watchtower, where you will be given a presentation and you can study an array of books, maps, and photographs. In the afternoon, we will come together to compare notes." Lyle looked up. "Any questions?"

I stared at him. Could I? *Should* I? Could it wait till tomorrow?

Before my brain had formulated an answer to the questions swimming around in my head, my hand had made up its mind and shot into the air.

Miss Platt looked at me. "Emily, you have a question for Lyle?"

My mouth opened and closed, unsure whose side to take—brain or hand. It chose the latter. "Are any of the shipwrecks, like, totally intact?" I asked.

Lyle frowned at me. "I don't understand. What do you mean?"

I gulped. "I mean, as in, do any of them look more ship, and less wreck?"

Lyle nodded. "Oh, yes. There is an enormous variety. Some are little more than a rusty, algae-covered engine. Others are practically entire ships that you would almost imagine could set sail and return home, were they not filled with water."

"Any tall ships?" I asked, my voice coming out like a croak.

Lyle looked at me. "Any what?" he asked sharply.

"Tall. Like big. With, maybe, say, three masts— really tall wooden things with dirty, torn sails. Long, shiny front deck. Maybe slightly above the water. Um. Anything like that at all . . . ?"

What was I doing? What was I saying? Everyone

had turned to stare at me. Even Aaron was looking at me as if I'd lost my mind and gone running off a cliff and out to sea to find it.

In the tightened air, Lyle held my eyes for one more second. Then he breathed in sharply through his nose and snapped, "No. None like that."

Before I had the chance to respond, he'd turned away and was addressing the whole group again. "Right. Enough questions. I'll see you tomorrow." And with that, he turned and walked away, leaving us to stare after him and wonder what on earth had just happened.

Miss Platt was the first to recover. She clapped her hands to get everyone's attention. "OK, children, you heard what Lyle said. Tomorrow morning, we'll meet back here at nine sharp for Shallows and Shipwrecks. Now then, Brightport, back to the cabin with me. Let's get cleaned up for dinner."

I stood up and looked out at the Shiprock group, gathering around Mr. Finsplash. Shona waved at me from the water as they turned away.

"See you in the morning," I mouthed, and she smiled before darting under the waves with the rest of the Shiprock kids.

I joined the others heading back to the cabin and tried not to think too much about the amount of weird that the last hour had contained. It would all make sense at some point. Surely it would.

I fell into step with Aaron and Mandy.

"Shallows and Shipwrecks, eh?" Aaron said. "Sounds like this week could be really fun."

"Mmm," I said unenthusiastically.

"What's up?" Mandy asked. "Don't you think it sounds good?"

"Yeah, of course . . ." I said.

"But?" Mandy pushed.

I shrugged. "I dunno."

Aaron nudged me. "Yes, you do. I know you. Come on, what's wrong? And what were all those weird questions about?"

"Not to mention Lyle's even weirder answer," Mandy added. "Did you see him? It was like he completely shut down."

I stopped walking, and they did the same. "Look, just hang back from the others a minute and I'll tell you," I said in a low voice.

We waited for everyone else to come past us before setting off again at a slower pace.

"Can I trust you?" I asked, glancing from one to the other as we walked.

"Of course you can!" Aaron blurted out right away. "How can you even ask me that after everything we've—"

"She's not asking you," Mandy interrupted. "She's asking me."

I didn't reply.

Mandy pulled on my arm. "Emily," she said as the three of us stopped and hung back even farther, "look at me."

I met her eyes.

"Making friends with you again, and meeting your new friends"—she nodded toward Aaron—"has been the best thing that's ever happened to me. Right?"

I held her eyes for a moment, wondering if there was a punch line coming. Something like, *Yeah, it was the best way to remind me what a bunch of losers you are!* I couldn't help it. Expecting Mandy to say something mean was a habit left over from the days when she and I had been sworn enemies.

"There's no punch line coming," Mandy said, spooking me out completely by how accurately she'd read my mind.

"I mean it," Mandy went on as we started walking again. "These last few months have been . . . They've been . . ." She laughed and shook her head. "Yeah, OK, I feel like a dork for saying it, but they've been *swishy!*"

I laughed, too. Hearing Mandy use that word was like, well, a bit like having a boiled egg with ice cream on top. It didn't quite go. I still liked it, though.

"I think she's trying to say you can trust her," Aaron put in.

Mandy laughed again. "Yeah. That's exactly what I'm trying to say. And you'd better get on with whatever it is you need to get off your chest because we'll be back at the cabin soon. So, come on. Spill."

"OK," I said. "If you're ready for a whole lot of weird, I've got something to tell you."

Aaron and Mandy listened while I told them what had happened out at sea.

"You said you thought it was a shipwreck," Mandy pointed out when I'd finished. "It sounds more like a ghost ship — especially with that scary woman. That is some kind of spooky!"

"I know. I don't know why I asked Lyle about shipwrecks. I think I was just desperate to find a way of looking at it that might make sense — that might make me *not* feel like some kind of freak who's seeing things."

"You're not any kind of freak," Aaron said. "Or at least if you are, then I am as well."

Mandy scratched her head. "Huh? Why's that?"

"Because I saw the ship, too."

Mandy turned back to me. "I thought you said you were with Shona."

"I was."

"Not just now," Aaron explained. "I saw it earlier. We saw it together."

"You *did* see it?" I checked. "You didn't just pretend to see it to make me feel better?"

"What? Why would I do that? Of course I saw it. Big ship, three huge masts, torn sails. Yeah, Em, I saw it."

I let out a breath that I felt as if I'd been holding for the last hour.

"And you think it's the same ship?" Mandy asked.

I nodded. "It looked the same to me. It even did the same disappearing act. I watched it for a while—maybe ten, fifteen minutes at most—and then, in the blink of an eye, it was gone."

"It's *got* to be a ghost ship," Mandy said. "No other explanation for it. Cool! I hope it comes back again!"

I bit my lip as I thought about this. "Yeah, but that's the thing. Even if it does, I don't know if you'll see it."

"True, we might be asleep or on the other side of the island," she agreed.

"No, not just that," I insisted. "Look. I was with Shona. She was *right there*—and she didn't see it. No one else has seen it."

"Except me," Aaron reminded me.

"Exactly. Just the two of us. Like, now, when I mentioned it in front of everyone. Don't you think that if anyone else had seen it, they'd have said something?"

Mandy let out a low whistle. "So you think it's only you guys who can even see this thing?"

I raised a shoulder. "I don't know," I admitted.

"But it's certainly looking that way," Aaron finished.

We walked along in silence for a bit. We were nearly back at the cabin, and everyone else had gone inside.

Mandy stopped at the door. "Look, let's keep this between ourselves," she said. "You'll be teased rotten if you go around saying you've seen a disappearing ghost ship. You know what . . . people . . . can be like."

I knew what she meant. She meant I knew what *she* had been like, before we'd become friends again. And she was right. I didn't want anyone to make me feel like I was a freak like that ever again.

"I agree. Just us and Shona," I said. "She's already part of this."

"And Seth," Aaron added.

I looked at him. "You're sure? He works for Neptune."

Aaron nodded. "I'm sure. He's not going to tell Neptune anything. He's here because he's our friend, and he's as loyal and trustworthy as you could get."

I had to admit, Aaron was right. Seth was the one who had helped save all of us from Neptune's evil twin last year. Maybe he'd help me save the woman on the ship.

"And he's kind of my best friend, I guess," Aaron mumbled in that cute way he does when he's feeling shy. It made me want to kiss him, but obviously I would never do that in front of Mandy!

"OK, so us, Shona, and Seth, but we don't tell anyone else," I said instead.

"Agreed," Mandy and Aaron said together.

"And tomorrow, when we're studying shipwrecks at the Watchtower, we'll examine every picture, every article, every bit of information we can find about shipwrecks," Aaron added.

Mandy grimaced. "I'm going to look like such a goody two-shoes," she said, a tiny shade of the old Mandy returning for a moment.

"Look, if you'd rather not—" I began.

She cut me off. "No! It's fine. The others can think what they like. We're in this together."

As we let ourselves into the cabin and got ready for dinner, I tried to take comfort from her words.

I decided that as long as I had my best friends with me, I wasn't going to let *anything* scare me. Not even a huge, disappearing ghost ship with torn sails and silent, screaming passengers.

I mean, why would that be scary?

Chapter Eight

*A*ll right, children, there isn't much space, so you'll have to be patient."

It was Monday morning, and Miss Platt was attempting to keep order while we shuffled around on the hill, ready to take turns to go into the Watchtower for our Shallows and Shipwrecks session.

"Three at a time on the ground floor for your presentation with Lyle. After that, you can go up to the observation deck. Before your turn, have a look around the outside of the Watchtower. There's plenty to see. Please, be careful at all times, and stay away from the edge of the cliffs."

I stood looking out to sea. Aaron came over to join me.

"Wish we could have done the session with the Shiprock class," he said. "Going out and seeing the shipwrecks for real would have been much better than just reading about them."

"Yeah," I agreed, although, after yesterday's experience, I was actually quite happy not to be exploring underwater shipwrecks up close.

Aaron leaned in and lowered his voice. "Actually, if I'm honest, I'm not too bothered."

"No? How come?"

He kicked a stone between his feet. "Well, you know . . ." he began.

I turned toward him. "I know what?"

Aaron kicked the stone again, this time firing it off the side of the hill. Then he looked at me. "I, um . . ."

Just then, Mandy called to us from the Watchtower. "Hey, guys! We're up."

Aaron pointed at Mandy, then at me. "That," he said. "This. I get to hang out with my pals. Come on, let's go."

And with that, he turned away—leaving me once again wondering if he was trying to tell me something. If it was about how he saw me only as one of his pals, I was quite happy being in the dark for now.

We joined Mandy at the door to the Watchtower.

"Remember, we need to find everything we can that might give us information on the ship," Mandy reminded us as we went inside.

"Yeah, and don't forget, after Lyle's talk, we can go upstairs to the observation level and have a look around there, too," Aaron added.

"Let's hope we find something. It's probably our best chance," I said quietly, crossing my fingers.

To our right there was a door with a PRIVATE! NO ENTRY! sign on it. Opposite, Lyle was sitting in an office.

"Come in and make yourselves comfortable," he said without looking up as he shuffled some papers around on his desk. "I'm just tidying up from the last talk. Give me two minutes and I'll give you a history of some of the ships that have been lost on the rocks around our beautiful island."

We scuttled into his office and stood awkwardly in front of his desk while he finished sorting his papers.

"OK. Ready. Sorry to keep you waiting," he said. As he looked at us, his expression changed. Correction: as he looked at *me,* it changed. It seemed as though whatever made his face face-shaped had suddenly lost its elastic, and whatever made it face-colored had been diluted with gray water.

"Oh," he said. "Oh. It's you." He quickly stood up and went over to the door. He glanced both ways, then softly closed it and came back into the room.

He gestured for us to sit on some stools in a corner of his office and pulled his chair away from his desk to join us in a small circle. "We need to be quick," he said. "The next group will be expecting to come in soon." Lyle pointed at me. "What's your name?"

"Me?" What had I done wrong?

"Yes. What's your name?"

"Emily," I said.

Lyle nodded sharply. "OK, so, Emily. These are your friends?"

"Yes."

"Good. You trust them?"

I glanced on either side of me at Aaron and Mandy. "Yes, I do," I said. "But I don't understand. Why are you asking all these questions? Aren't you supposed to be giving us a talk?"

Lyle waved my question away. "The other groups, yes. Not you. You're different."

I swallowed. "Have I done something wrong?" I asked. Had he found out about Aaron and me going off on our own? Was he going to tell the teachers? Could I not even manage a week without getting myself into trouble of one sort or another?

"No! No, no, not at all. Quite the opposite. Look, we haven't got long. Tell me everything."

We stared at him. What was he talking about?

"Tell you everything about *what*?" Aaron asked.

Lyle stared me straight in the eye. "The . . . the ship." His voice cracked as he said the word.

"The ship? Which ship?" I asked, playing for time. Was this a trick? What was he trying to do? Make me say something impossible so he could tell me how crazy it was?

Lyle's gaze burned into me. "The ship you saw. The one you mentioned in front of everyone. Describe it. I want every detail."

For a moment, I pictured the ship as I'd swum around it—the hull, the decks, the sails. The woman.

"I . . ." I began. Where to start? And *should* I start? I mean, we'd agreed I wouldn't tell anyone about it.

"Why do you want to know?" Aaron broke in. Good. Someone needed to be in charge here. I certainly wasn't.

Lyle glanced at him. "Research," he replied sharply. "We need to keep records of all the ships that come through here." There was something about the way he said it—he sounded as wooden as a ship's deck.

We had no idea *why* we'd seen the ship, but if Aaron and I were the only ones who could see it, that made us valuable—and until we knew more about Lyle's motives, who knew what kind of value we had to him? In the past I'd been spied on, lied to, and even kidnapped by Neptune—all because I was a semi-mer and because of what that meant

I could do. I wasn't about to let that happen again. Plus, we'd first seen the ship when we were on the part of the island we'd been told was out-of-bounds. There was no way I was going to willingly get myself into trouble by admitting that!

"She didn't see anything," Aaron said firmly, leaning right across me and answering Lyle directly. He stared pointedly at me. "You were just kidding around, weren't you?"

Before I had the chance to answer, Mandy broke in, too. "We put her up to it," she said. Then she forced out a laugh that sounded like a hyena having a sneezing fit. "Yeah," she went on. "Emily's really into, um, like, stories and things. And she's got a good imagination. All the teachers say so." She turned to me. "Don't they, Emily?"

Actually, at least that part was true. "Mm, yes, they do," I agreed.

"So, we said she had to ask a question that used her imagination," Aaron put in. "Just for fun. Making a joke, you know."

I wasn't a hundred percent sure what Mandy and Aaron were getting at, but I knew they were protecting me, and I suddenly felt overwhelmed with relief and gratitude.

Until I saw Lyle's face. It looked as if a door had closed across his eyes. "Fun," he said, nodding slowly. "A joke. Making a joke." His voice sounded like gravel.

Then he got up out of his chair and shuffled over to the door. He turned the handle. "You'd better leave," he said, opening the door.

Leave? We'd only just gotten there!

The three of us looked at one another, unsure what to do — or what was happening.

"I'm sorry," Lyle said. "I'm just not feeling too well today. I thought . . ." His voice broke. "I thought . . ." he tried again. Then he shook his head and cleared his throat. "Please tell Miss Platt you're all welcome to visit the observation deck for as long as you like, but I won't be conducting any more talks today."

There was something about his tone that made it very clear this wasn't up for discussion. We awkwardly got up from our stools and shuffled across his tiny office toward the door. Lyle stood there, his hand tight on the handle, his face turned down toward the floor. For a split second, something about his posture made me want to take it all back and tell him the truth.

Then he looked up and his eyes met mine. "Just go," he said. "Please."

Even if I'd wanted to tell him, I couldn't. Not now. There was no doubt that the only thing he needed from us right then was space. Which, to be honest, was absolutely fine with me. All of this was *way* too strange for my liking, and I was happy to get out and leave him to it. I started making my way out of his office.

Five more seconds and I would have been gone.

A glance in the opposite direction and it would have been fine.

A different way around the desk and I would never have known.

But none of those things happened.

Instead, I walked around the back of Lyle's desk, glanced at a photo in a frame—and my world tilted.

The photo was of a woman. A woman I'd glimpsed very recently. A woman whose face had been burned into my thoughts ever since I'd seen it.

It made no sense. It surely couldn't be true. And yet it was.

The woman with the big green eyes and the straggly red hair—the one I'd seen screaming inside the vanishing ghost ship out at sea—was now smiling brightly at me from a picture in a frame on Lyle's desk.

Chapter Nine

I stumbled out of the office.

"Weirdo," Mandy hissed.

"Come on, let's go upstairs. We'll probably find more useful stuff up there anyway," Aaron replied. "I'll just go tell Miss Platt that there won't be any more talks. I'll meet you up there."

I followed Mandy upstairs in a trance.

"Em, are you OK?" Aaron asked once we were all up at the observation deck.

"You've gone white," Mandy added. "Are you sick?"

Was I? Maybe I was. Perhaps it was a hallucination. Either way, I knew I couldn't keep it to myself. I had to tell them what I'd seen.

"There was a photo on the desk," I said, my voice coming out in such a quivery shake that it sounded as if I were singing.

Aaron held my eyes and nodded for me to go on. "I didn't see it," he said. "What was it? Was it something that upset you?"

"No. Well, yes. I don't know. It . . . it was a woman."

"Oh, yeah, I saw it on my way in," Mandy said. "Long red hair, smiley eyes, quite pretty?"

"Mm-hm, that was the one."

They both waited for me to go on. "I, um, I've seen her before," I mumbled. "On the ship. Out there. Out at sea."

Mandy's jaw dropped open.

"You're kidding!" Aaron breathed.

"I'm not. I mean, I *might* be wrong. . . ."

"But you don't think you are," Mandy finished.

I shook my head. "No. I'm positive it was her."

Aaron whistled. "That is seriously freaky," he muttered.

I bristled at his words. Was he calling me a freak?

"Not you," he added quickly. "Her. Him. This place. What is going on around here?"

I shrugged. I had *no* idea what was going on around here.

Mandy broke the silence. She was standing by

the door that led into the observation room. "Look, we're in the best place to find out," she said. "If there's a spooky ship somewhere near this island, surely we'll see it from here—a watchtower with windows all the way around it."

"And if there's information about the ship, it'll be in here if it's anywhere," Aaron added. "Lyle told us there were lots of reference books and maps here."

"OK, so we find out what we can here," I said.

"And we don't give up till we've searched every corner of the place," Mandy finished.

Aaron led the way. "Agreed. OK, let's go."

Half an hour later, we'd used every telescope and pair of binoculars in the room to scan the ocean from the closest shores all the way out to the horizon. Nothing. The ship was definitely not out there.

We disregarded the folders labeled FLORA AND FAUNA, bypassed the ones named FLOTSAM AND JETSAM, ignored BUTTERFLIES AND BUGS, and a quick flip through the ones titled REEFS AND ROCKS showed us that even those were of no use to us.

Finally, we found what we were looking for— three whole shelves of folders labeled SHIPS, WRECKS, AND LOCAL LANDMARKS.

"Bingo!" Mandy whispered.

Aaron pulled out three folders and put them on the table in the middle of the room. "Come on," he said. "Let's get to work."

We flicked through the papers, ignoring our classmates who came and went around us. Mostly, they ran straight for the telescopes, looked out to sea for a bit, then wandered around picking up binoculars and walkie-talkies before getting bored and leaving us to it.

Mandy was halfway through a new folder when she nudged me. "Em . . ." she said.

"Uh-huh." I looked up from a page entitled "Some Pleasure Boats That Have Visited Our Shores in Recent Years."

"What did the ship look like again?" Mandy asked.

"Big," I said. "Really big. And Long. With a dark-blue hull, three masts, and sails that—"

"Did it look anything like this?" Mandy held her folder up to show me the pictures she'd found.

It looked *exactly* like it. I couldn't speak.

Aaron glanced up from what he was doing. He saw the page Mandy was holding, saw my face, and came to my side. "That's the one! Em, it is, isn't it?"

I held my hand out for the folder. "Let me see."

Mandy passed it across to me. There were three pictures on the page. I studied them, one by one. The first showed the ship from a distance. You could see the bowsprit jutting proudly forward, the three tall masts behind. I couldn't see the sails because they were wrapped up and rolled away. But from what I could see, this looked like the same ship.

The second photo showed a closer side view — the long, sleek hull, dark blue and rising outward at the sides. Again, the sails were wrapped up. They looked much neater than the scrappy bits of cloth I'd seen — but everything else looked more or less the same.

I was about to say this was definitely the ship, but when I glanced at the third photo, I wasn't so sure. This one showed a detail of the front of the hull. The netted hammock was the same. The mermaid/dragon figurehead was there, looking just as spooky. But the lettering along the front of the hull — something about it was different. On this third picture, I could clearly see the ship's name: *Prosperous*. Was that the same name? It sounded familiar but not quite right. What was different about it?

Underneath the photos, an extract from a newspaper article had been stuck onto the page. There was just one paragraph of text:

Prosperous was built in 1857. It was one of many ships built during the Golden Age of Sail that were intended to be efficient commercial sailing ships. *Prosperous* carried

people, goods, and mail for almost forty years until its illustrious career was brought to an abrupt end with its tragic wrecking in 1893.

I stopped reading as my eyes glazed over.

"Tragic wrecking?" Aaron murmured.

"So it *was* a ghost ship!" Mandy replied. "I mean, I know I joked about it, but I didn't really think—"

"No. Wait." I stopped them both. "Look at this."

Beneath the newspaper extract was another piece of paper. This one contained two sentences:

To mark the centennial of the demise of *Prosperous*, a replica was built in 1993. *Prosperous II* serves mostly as a luxury passenger ship, although it also carries some specialized cargo from time to time.

Prosperous II—that was the name of the ship I'd seen!

"The replica," I said, pointing at the words on the page that were now beginning to swim beneath my gaze. "That was the one I saw."

"You're sure?" Aaron asked.

I nodded. "It had the name on its hull. It was definitely *Prosperous II*. Apart from that, it looked exactly like this ship."

"So we've found it!" Mandy said. "Wow!"

"Yeah," I agreed.

Aaron was stroking his chin. "But that's . . . I mean, OK, let's look at this logically . . ."

I almost laughed. "Logically?" I asked. "How are we supposed to be logical about any of this?"

"Well, let's look at the facts. If *Prosperous II* was the ship you saw . . ."

"Which I'm positive it was."

"Then it wasn't a shipwreck."

"Unless the replica one was wrecked, too," Mandy put in.

Aaron tilted his head and frowned. "Yeah, I guess."

"But that's highly unlikely," Mandy conceded. She flicked over a couple more pages. "And surely it would have said something in here if it had been. These folders seem pretty thorough."

"OK, so let's assume that *Prosperous II* didn't meet the same fate as the original *Prosperous*," Aaron went on.

"Then we know that the ship I saw wasn't a shipwreck and wasn't a ghost ship, either," I said.

Aaron nodded. "Correct."

"So what *was* it, then?" Mandy asked.

I looked at her. "I guess that's what we need to find out."

Aaron gazed around the room. "We need a computer," he said. "We need to Google '*Prosperous II.*' There's bound to be some information on Wikipedia or something."

"You're right," Mandy agreed. "I can hardly believe there's no Internet on this entire island. I've tried to get reception on my phone about a hundred times."

"Wait." I'd had a thought. "There is a computer. Just one. Maybe it's connected to the Internet."

"Where is it?" Aaron asked.

"Lyle's office."

"Of course!" Mandy's eyes beamed. "It *is* connected. I remember noticing a wire attached to a modem and thinking how quaint that it had to be wired up like that for Internet access. It's probably the only place on the whole island where we can get online."

"That's fantastic!" Aaron said. "We just need to get back in there."

"Hmm," I said. "That's not going to be the easiest task in the world, given the way our last encounter ended."

"What, you mean the fact that he kicked us out of his office and then locked himself away in there and said he wasn't going to talk to anyone else all day?" Aaron asked. "You think perhaps now isn't the best time for us to go back in and ask him to do us a favor?"

I gave him a playful punch in the side. "Maybe not," I agreed. "We need to distract him, somehow. Get him out of the office so we can sneak in and use his computer."

Mandy was looking out of the window. "Hold on," she said. "I think I've got an idea."

Aaron and I watched from upstairs till we saw Lyle leave the Watchtower with Mandy. We were waiting quite a while. I guess it took quite a bit of persuasion for Mandy to get him to talk to her at all, let alone leave his office.

"Yes!" Aaron suddenly exclaimed. "She's done it. Look."

I glanced out the window in time to see Mandy leading Lyle along the cliff top toward a clump of bright-yellow flowers a few minutes' walk away. Mandy had seen these from the window, and the plan was that she would ask Lyle as many questions as she could think of—about these, and the island's plant life in general—to keep him talking and away from the Watchtower. While she was doing that, we'd use his computer to get online and find out anything we could about *Prosperous II.*

"Come on, let's go," I said. We scurried down the stairs to the ground floor, past the PRIVATE! NO ENTRY! door, and headed to the office. Luckily, Lyle had left it unlocked and we sneaked inside.

I followed Aaron around to Lyle's chair behind his desk. I couldn't help glancing at the photo of the woman in the frame. It was definitely the woman I'd seen through the porthole; I was sure of it.

Aaron and I both perched on Lyle's chair, and Aaron typed *"Prosperous II"* into the search bar. The first page brought up links to a couple of art galleries, an Egyptian temple, three banks, and a quote from the Bible.

"Hang on." I reached for the keyboard, this time typing, "Tall ship named *Prosperous II.*"

"That's better," Aaron said as the page loaded with links to tall ships. There were a lot of them.

"Wow. Seems like *Prosperous* is quite a popular name for a boat," I murmured as we clicked on each link to see what it said. There were all sorts of ships — mostly modern ones, but a few older ones. None that looked like the one I'd seen.

"Try just searching for pictures," I suggested.

Aaron clicked the IMAGES tab at the top of the page — and finally, we were getting somewhere. The page loaded with row after row of photos of ships — mostly tall ships, and many of them looking like the one I'd seen. I studied them all, scrolling down, row by row.

Finally, on about the twentieth row, I saw it. I jabbed a finger at the screen. "That's it!"

"Are you sure?"

"Positive. The writing on the hull looks exactly the same, and that dragon/mermaid figurehead would be hard to mistake. That's the ship, definitely."

Aaron clicked on the picture. More photos came up. Underneath them was a link with "Prosper Vacations. Go straight to website" written beside it. He clicked the link.

While we waited for the page to load, I got up and looked out the window. Lyle was still outside with Mandy. She was pointing to a tree halfway down the hillside. Lyle had his hands in his pockets and looked impatient to get away. *Keep him talking, Mandy. Just a couple more minutes . . .*

"It's a passenger ship," Aaron said.

"Like the original one?"

"Kind of. That one carried cargo, too, didn't it?"

I tried to remember what the information in the folder had said. "Yes, I think so. Commercial goods and passengers." I came back over to the computer and looked over his shoulder.

"This one is run by a vacation company." Aaron clicked another button and a list of dates and prices came up. He whistled as he looked at the figures.

"A very exclusive vacation company, by the look of it," I said.

"I'll say." He clicked on SEPTEMBER, and we studied the dates. "It sets sail every two weeks. And if this information is up-to-date, it looks like the most recent trip left last Monday, a week ago."

"Does it say where it left from?" I asked.

"Can't see anything."

We studied the page. "Look—there, in the top

corner." I pointed at a square that contained a small picture of a map.

Aaron clicked the picture and the image opened up to full-size. A squiggly red line on the map indicated what was presumably the ship's course. At various points along the line, there were numbers from one to fourteen.

"That must be where the ship is on each day," I mused.

"I guess."

"So last Monday was day one." I followed the line, charting the ship's journey. The first two days it skirted along the coast. The next two were spent out at sea. I got as far as day five.

"Aaron," I said, my voice coming out like the rasp of a dying man. I couldn't manage more than one word. Instead I just pointed at the number.

"Day five," Aaron said. "What about it?"

I took the mouse and clicked to enlarge the map further. The area around the DAY FIVE mark filled the screen. The red line ran alongside an island—and from the picture, there was no doubt about which island it was.

Aaron let out a long breath. "It was due to arrive here," he said.

"Yeah," I agreed.

But the fact that the mysterious ship had been due to pass Fivebays Island last Friday wasn't the weird thing. The *weird* thing was that it *should* have passed by quickly and moved on that same day.

So why hadn't it continued its journey? Why wasn't it three hundred miles out at sea by now? And *why* were Aaron and I the only ones who could see it?

The questions beat against my mind, mixing together with the picture of the woman's face and her words: "Help us! Help us!"

I had no idea what any of this meant, but I knew one thing: the ship was somehow stuck—and until we could figure out how to free it, nothing else on this field trip was going to hold one iota of my attention.

Chapter Ten

*E*m!" Aaron tugged at my sleeve. He'd stood up and was looking out the window. "Lyle's coming back. We need to go."

I shook myself out of my thoughts.

"Quick, close the web pages and let's get out of here," he said. I clicked the CLOSE button on all the pages we'd visited and prayed Lyle wouldn't check the browser history and realize that someone had used his computer.

Aaron was by the door, looking out. "Ready?" he whispered. "We'll have to go upstairs till he's back in his office. If we walk out now, it'll look too obvious."

We scurried out of the office and up the spiral staircase just in time to see Lyle come back into the building, go into his office, and close the door behind him.

Once his office door was closed, I let out a breath as my knees almost buckled under me.

"You OK?" Aaron asked.

I shrugged. I had no idea whether or not I was OK. I didn't have too much time to think about it, though; someone was coming up the stairs.

"There you are!" Mandy said. "Did you find anything?"

"Oh, yeah," Aaron replied, "we found something!"

She beckoned us downstairs. "Great! Tell me about it on the way to lunch. Miss Platt says we're joining Shiprock for a picnic at Sandy Bay."

Aaron and I filled Mandy in as we made our way over to meet the others.

"So where do we go with this now?" Mandy asked as we arrived at the beach, echoing the question lurking in the back of my mind.

"I have no idea," I admitted. We wandered down to the water's edge, where the Shiprock kids were arriving. "Maybe Shona or Seth will have some ideas."

We reached the shallow waves lapping softly onto the sand. "We'll tell them everything over lunch,"

Aaron said. "Surely, between the five of us, we should be able to come up with *some* kind of plan."

Shona and Seth listened to the whole story as we ate our lunch and splashed in the soft waves.

Shona's eyes had gone all wide and watery, like they always do when we start getting involved in an adventure. "This week is turning out to be so much more exciting than I'd thought it would be," she breathed.

I couldn't help wincing. She hadn't seen the woman on the ship — her eyes scared and desperate.

I shook the image out of my mind and tried to think about the smiling version on Lyle's desk instead. But that just made me confused. Who *was* this woman?

As if I'd spoken the question out loud, Mandy suddenly blurted out, "Do you think she's his wife?"

We all turned to look at her.

"Lyle's wife," she went on. "I mean, she's in a picture frame on his desk. Don't you think that makes it quite likely?"

Mandy was right. And that would fit with the way Lyle had questioned me about the boat.

"It was when I said I hadn't seen anything that

he went all weird and said he didn't want to talk to us anymore," I mused.

Shona's eyes had gone super sparkly. "Of course! She's Lyle's wife! She must be!"

"Even if she is, you know that doesn't make this some kind of romantic love story!" I snapped.

Shona looked as if I'd slapped her.

"I'm sorry," I said quickly. "Sorry. I just—"

"No, *I'm* sorry," Shona said. "You're right. I'm getting carried away, being excited by a mystery, but you're the one who's seen all the scary things. I'm an idiot."

"You're not an idiot," I said. "But thanks."

Seth was frowning, as though he were thinking hard. "Even if she is his wife, it doesn't give us any more answers. If anything, it only raises more questions."

"Exactly," I agreed. "And I would love to try to find some answers without creating *more* questions."

Seth glanced at Aaron, then at me. "Well, you know what you have to do, don't you?"

"I . . ."

Mandy broke in. "She has to talk to Lyle."

"I do?"

Seth nodded. "He's the only person who can tell you if the woman in the photo is his wife."

"And if she is, he's the only person who might know how she got onto that ship," Mandy added.

They were right.

Aaron nodded. "I'll come with you," he said. "We'll figure out exactly what to say. We'll do it carefully, and we'll do it together."

I looked at him for a moment. His face was set and serious. "OK," I agreed. "Thank you."

"Good luck," Seth said. "I'll check in with you in a few days to see how you're doing."

"In a few days? What do you mean?" Aaron asked.

"Unfortunately, duty calls."

"Seth's been summoned back to work," Shona explained. "Seems Neptune's getting his tail in a tizzy without him."

"I'm heading off this evening on the high tide. I'm hoping I can come back before the end of the week, but you know Neptune. I'm sure he'll have a hundred urgent matters that need dealing with before then."

"We'll miss you," Aaron said.

I was still lost in my thoughts about Lyle and the ship, so I only half took in what Seth was saying. But something about what he'd said was nudging at me. "When's high tide?" I asked.

"About six-ish. Just before. Why?"

It had been high tide when I'd seen the ship in the channel yesterday, which would have been about an hour earlier than today's high tide. What about the first time? When had that been?

"Aaron, when did we find that chair?" I asked.

Aaron turned to me. "Huh? Yesterday!"

"No. I mean, what time?"

He frowned. "Can't remember. It was in the morning. Maybe eleven? Eleven thirty?"

I nodded.

"Why?" Mandy asked.

"It's nothing," I said. But *was* it nothing? If high tide had been just after five yesterday, low tide would have been about six hours earlier—which would have been around the same time that Aaron and I saw the ship. Was it significant? Could the tides have anything to do with us seeing it? If so, did that mean we might be able to see it again at high tide tonight? Did I *want* to see it again?

Aaron was looking at me, with a *You sure you're OK?* expression on his face.

"What are you thinking?" Shona asked.

I shrugged. "It's just . . . the ship. I think it was high tide when I saw it the second time."

Shona jumped in the waves, her tail flicking a bit of water in my eye. I rubbed it away. "It was!" she said. "Because, remember, we had to meet up just after high tide, and we were the last ones to the beach. So I figure it was probably exactly high tide while we were out there."

"And that's why you were asking about when we found the chair," Aaron mused.

"But if that was in the morning, it couldn't have been high tide then, too," Mandy said.

"No," Seth agreed, "but it could have been *low* tide."

"Exactly," I said. "I think it might have been on the low and high tides that I saw it. Not that that helps us understand any more about it."

"Maybe not," Aaron admitted, "but any connections we can make are better than none at all."

I nodded. "Yeah, let's hope so."

"I've got an idea," Shona said. "Let's meet later, when Seth has to go. He leaves on the high tide, so if we're right that the ship has got something to do with the tides, perhaps you'll see it again."

"It's worth a try," Aaron said. "Maybe we could swim the first part of his journey with him. Head out toward where you saw the ship."

A shiver ran down my spine, like a cold piece of seaweed brushing against me. Did I *want* to see the ship up close again? The people? The woman?

On the other hand, could I really leave all these questions unanswered?

"OK, it sounds like a plan," I said eventually. "But what about you, Mandy?"

"I'll cover for you back at the cabin. We'll have free time then, but if you're not back when we sit down for dinner at seven, I'll come up with an excuse for you."

I caught Mandy's eye. "Thank you," I said—and I hoped she knew I was thanking her for much more than just making up an excuse for us to skip dinner.

She held my look for a moment. "Yeah, it's cool," she replied.

"Swishy!" Shona said. "Then, after dinner, you guys can go to see Lyle."

"All of which means that by tomorrow morning, one way or another, we should have at least a few answers to all these mysterious questions," Aaron said.

"All right, children. You've had long enough for your lunch." Miss Platt was standing up and wiping sand from her skirt. "We're going to form interschool groups for this afternoon's activity. First of all, we'd like you to share what you've found out this morning."

I smiled at the others. Well, we'd already done that. Maybe we'd get the afternoon off.

"And once you've done that," Miss Platt continued, dashing my hopes of a free afternoon playing with my friends, "we're going to meet at Pebble Bay, where we will start our geological study of the island's interesting rock formations."

"You're kidding," Mandy muttered. "Could they have thought of *anything* more boring than that?"

As if she'd heard us, Miss Platt added, "Remember, this is a school trip. It's not a vacation. You are here to have a good time, but also to learn. Now, form groups, people—and this time, we want you to get together with people you haven't teamed up with before. As well as everything else, we're getting to know one another this week." She paused and shot a look in our direction before adding, "If you join up with the same group of friends for every activity, you are hardly pursuing the cause of bringing two worlds together."

"She means us," Mandy grumbled.

"Seems like it," Shona agreed. "I guess I'll see you later."

"Meet you at six, at Deep Blue Bay?" I suggested. "Mandy will cover for us at the cabin, and the rest of us will swim out with Seth from there."

"Sounds like a plan," Aaron agreed as we broke up the group to find new people to talk to.

As we parted company and I teamed up with Gemma from my class, and Meryn and Gabe from Shiprock, I couldn't help wondering if I was looking forward to meeting up with everyone again later—or dreading it.

The afternoon passed surprisingly quickly. Not that studying the geological formation of an island is interesting—but hanging out with new people and taking my mind off all the weird stuff was actually quite refreshing.

Which meant that six o'clock came around fast, and it was soon time to start facing all the question marks again.

Aaron and I went over the plan with Mandy one last time as we walked to Deep Blue Bay.

"So, remember, if you come in late, you say you lost your shoes at Sandy Bay and had to go back for them," Mandy said.

"And I went with her so I could help her over the rocks at the top of the beach," Aaron suggested.

I gave him a *Really?* kind of look.

"What?" Aaron held his arms out in a helpless shrug. "It's rough ground over there, and if you had no shoes on, you'd *need* some help."

I laughed and decided not to point out that I'd already walked pretty much the length of the island without shoes on.

"Besides, I need *some* kind of excuse to be with you," he insisted. "And anyway, we'll probably be back by then."

"OK, whatever. We'll go with that," I conceded.

We'd reached Deep Blue Bay. Mandy pointed out to sea.

"Look — there they are."

Shona and Seth had popped up from under the water and were waving at us from the middle of the bay.

"See you soon, Seth!" Mandy called to them, waving back. "Good luck with Neptune!"

Seth gave Mandy a salute, and Shona beckoned us to join them. "It's high tide in fifteen minutes," she called up. "We'd better get going."

I turned to Mandy. "Thank you—for everything."

She waved off my thanks. "OK, I'm heading back to the cabin. See you later. Just be careful, OK?"

"We will," I promised.

We piled up our shoes behind a rock. We'd already put our swimwear on underneath our clothes.

"Ready?" Aaron asked as we walked to the edge of the bay and prepared to dive in.

My stomach did a tiny twirl. Yes, it was spooky. Yes, the ship was surrounded by more question marks than portholes. And yes, the mysterious woman had haunted my thoughts ever since I'd seen her.

But this was an *adventure*. No matter what else happened, I was pretty sure we could guarantee it would be a hundred times more exciting than anything that had ever happened on any other Brightport geography field trip.

"You bet." I smiled. "Let's go."

Chapter Eleven

We'd been swimming for about ten minutes. It was nearly high tide, and we'd reached the channel where I'd seen the boat yesterday.

"This is definitely where you were last time?" Aaron asked.

"Yeah, I think so, although, to be honest, with all the twists and turns, it looks pretty similar all the way along."

Shona pointed at a bunch of rocks heaped into a dome that looked like an underwater igloo. "It's the same place," she said. "I remember that."

A moment later, everything fell still—just as it had the day before. Fish stopped moving; seaweed stopped swaying.

"Slack tide," Seth said quietly.

"Slack tide? What's that?" I asked.

"It's the time in between the tide coming in and turning around to go back out. It happens at high tide."

"Or the other way around," Shona added. "You get slack tide at low tide, too. It's basically the period where the sea pauses between doing one thing and turning around to do the opposite."

"I've never felt it like this before, though," Seth went on. "This *still*. It's as if the whole world has stopped, not just the tide."

Seth was right. It did feel like that—and it had felt exactly the same way the day before, too.

I was about to respond when something stopped me. Two things, actually. The first was Aaron tugging on my arm and saying, "Emily, look." The second was what I saw when I turned to see what he was pointing at.

The ship.

Right there in front of us, just like before—only something was different. Then it had been as real as anything—so real that I couldn't believe Shona hadn't seen it. Now it was barely visible—a pale, faded, watered-down version of the same ship. It was almost transparent. I felt I could swim through it.

Together, we swam toward the ship. At least, we tried to. One moment, it was there; the next, it had faded so much that it was barely a shadow.

I reached a hand out as we approached the disappearing ship and tried to touch it. With a tingling, buzzing feeling in the ends of my fingers, my hand went right through the ship's hull.

I gasped and jumped back, my tail flicking so hard to get me away from there that it created a cloud of bubbles.

"What's going on?" I whispered.

"Was it like this yesterday?" Aaron asked.

"No. It was absolutely solid. It was alive — a ship with sails and decks and people and — wait!" I pulled Aaron to the side of the ship, and we snaked along the edge of the channel. "The woman, she was in a porthole somewhere around the middle. Let's see if she's still there."

We swam past the portholes. Yesterday, I'd seen inside them — small cabins, each with a bed and a closet. Today, all we could see was darkness inside every one.

We came to the one where I'd seen the woman. "This was it," I said, flicking my tail to hold me back. I nudged Aaron forward. "You first."

Aaron swam up to the porthole and looked inside. "Just darkness, like the others," he said.

I swam alongside him, and we peered through the glass together. Aaron was right. There was only darkness. Except . . . as I stared into the darkness, shapes began to emerge.

"Aaron, look over there!" I jabbed a finger at the glass, careful not to touch it.

"What am I looking at?" Aaron scrunched up his face and stared into the room. "It's just murky gloom, like the others."

"Right at the back," I insisted.

"The back of what? I can't see anything. I can hardly even see the ship."

"The back of the room," I said, less confidently. Why couldn't he see it? Yes, it was dark and murky and the sight was fading as I watched, but I could still see it clearly enough. Was I imagining it? "The bed . . . the . . ."

I stopped. I couldn't say anything else. Couldn't speak. She was there. The woman. Sitting on the side of the bed, her head in her hands, slumped as if she'd given up.

I wanted to swim as far away as I could—and yet I was transfixed. "The woman," I whispered without taking my eyes off her. "Over there on the bed."

In that moment, as if she had heard me, the woman raised her head. Almost lifeless, almost ghostlike, she left her bed and seemed to float toward the porthole.

"I can't see anything," Aaron insisted, his voice starting to sound agitated. "Even the ship is disappearing. It's almost gone."

I could still see the ship. It was fading rapidly, but it was still there—just. And so was she. She met my eyes and reached out a hand toward me. I held my hand up to the porthole, for some reason no longer afraid to touch it. My fingers tingled so hard, it felt as if they were being prodded by a hundred needles. I ignored the feeling and flattened my hand so I was holding my palm against the window. The woman did the same.

This time I didn't feel glass. I felt a hand: flesh and bone, warm against my palm. I stared as her eyes met mine.

And then, a second later, it had changed. In an instant, as if they had never been there at all, the window, the woman, and the ship were gone.

"What happened?" Aaron was spinning around in a circle like a shoal of hungry fish, his tail flapping frantically. "Where did it go?"

I looked around, too. We were still in the channel, but it was now empty. The stillness had been replaced by a soft current. Seaweed stroked the tip of my tail. Fish darted by in small groups, like commuters just off work and hurrying home.

"It's gone," I said. It wasn't the most helpful reply in the world, but what else did I have?

"There you are!" Shona rounded a corner and swam toward us. "Are you OK?"

"Did we disappear?" Aaron asked her.

Shona scowled. "Not exactly."

"What do you mean?" I said.

Seth was beside her. "Well, you were there, but sort of not *really* there," he told us. "It's hard to explain. It was as though you were in another dimension or something."

"It was weird," Shona added—as if we didn't already know that.

"Look. I'm really sorry, but I have to go," Seth said. "I don't want to risk Neptune's temper if I'm late."

He had my sympathy. I'd been on the receiving end of Neptune's bad moods enough times to know that it wasn't fun.

"I'll see if I can find out anything that could help and will send word with a messenger if I do," Seth went on. "I hate to leave you like this, but . . ."

"It's fine," Aaron said. "We understand."

We said our good-byes to Seth and tried not to watch or listen as he and Shona said theirs—except for one bit that I couldn't help overhearing.

"I hope everything's OK with Neptune," Shona said. "And he doesn't give you a hard time for having had a couple of days away."

"He won't," Seth assured her. "And if he does, I'll tell him I'm entitled to a couple of days off . . . with my girlfriend."

Then Seth was gone, and the three of us turned back to the island.

"We saw it again," I told Shona. I didn't really

132

want to pull her out of the happy glow that she suddenly had around her now that Seth had called her his girlfriend, but this *was* what we'd come out here for — and I couldn't really focus on anything else.

"The ship?" Shona asked. I nodded. "What about the woman? Did you see her again, too?"

"Yes."

"No," Aaron said at the same moment. He looked at me. "Emily saw her. I was looking in the exact same place, but I couldn't see her. Emily could see the ship for longer than I could, too."

"Wow, that's . . ." Shona's voice trailed away. I didn't blame her. I mean, what exactly could she say? That's completely freaky? That's impossible? That's absolutely beyond ever explaining in a million years?

It didn't matter what she thought. Whatever else was going on, I knew one thing: we weren't going to figure it out by hanging around in a deserted channel out at sea.

"Come on," I said, starting to swim back the way we'd come. "If we go now, we'll probably get back in time for dinner." And then, because Shona was my best friend and I wanted her to be happy even if I was a bag of anxious confusion, I gave her a hug and said, "And you can talk about your boyfriend all the way back."

I even managed to half listen as Shona happily

talked about Seth while the three of us swam back to the island, to the others, and to a meal that my stomach was way too jittery for me to even *think* about eating.

Aaron and I filed out of the dining room with everyone else. He'd insisted I eat, so I'd forced some food down my throat and tried my best to chitchat with the others about any old thing. But I'd had enough now.

"Let's get out of here," I said, pulling him outside with me.

We made our way onto the road and started walking toward the woods. I'd have been happy just to go and sit in the middle of the trees and stare into space, not talking to anyone or thinking about anything, but I knew that wasn't going to happen. And I knew that we weren't really heading for the woods, either. We were heading toward the house in front of us: Lyle's house.

We stopped walking. We were almost directly in front of Lyle's front door. I looked at Aaron. "Come on," I said. "Let's get this over with."

We walked up the path in silence.

Aaron turned to me. "Ready?" he asked.

I shrugged. "Ready as I'll ever be," I replied, and knocked on the door.

We heard shuffling sounds inside. A few moments later, Lyle opened the door. He looked dreadful—even by *his* standards. His eyes were like black holes, his shirt was hanging out of his pants, and his hair was ruffled and messy.

"What do you want?" he asked.

"Um, well," I began, "we don't want to bother you—"

"Well, don't, then." Lyle turned to go back inside.

"But we have come to talk to you," I added firmly.

Lyle paused for a moment, and then he looked right at me and nodded—as if he knew what we wanted to talk about, as if he'd been expecting it even though he'd pretended he hadn't. Then he turned away and went inside. Leaving the door open for us, he called over his shoulder, "You'd better come in, then. And close the door behind you."

We did both.

"Take a seat." Lyle waved a hand carelessly across his living room.

I tried not to look at the dirty plates piled everywhere with half-eaten meals going moldy on them. Lyle must have seen me trying not to look, because he scrambled around, picking up the dishes and taking them into the kitchen.

"I wasn't expecting visitors," he said by way of explanation.

"It's fine," Aaron said brightly. "We didn't even notice, did we, Em?"

"Not at all," I lied as I stared around the room and wondered briefly if he might have been the victim of a burglary.

Aaron and I found a relatively untouched spot on the sofa and sat down. As I sat, my eyes fell on the dresser at the side of the room—and I no longer cared about or noticed *anything* else.

I stood up, walked over to the dresser, and picked up a framed photo as Lyle came back into the room.

It was a wedding picture—a smiling couple. On the left, dressed in a crisp white suit, was Lyle. He had such a huge smile that I could barely recognize him as the man in front of me now. The woman—also smiling brightly, her long red hair flowing over her shoulders and touching the top of a beautiful white wedding dress—was the woman whose face had barely left my thoughts for two days.

I put the photo down and turned to Lyle. "I've seen her," I said before I could stop myself.

"You've what?"

"I ... I've seen her," I repeated, realizing, somewhat belatedly, that perhaps I should have tried to think of a gentle way of breaking the news to him.

"Lowenna?" His voice broke as he said the word, as if the word itself broke him. He cleared his throat.

"You saw Lowenna?" he asked again, his words like splintered glass.

As he said her name, I had a vision of her the first time I'd seen her, fists pounding against the porthole. "I'm a winner," I'd thought she was calling, and couldn't understand why she'd be saying that. Now I realized that she hadn't been saying "I'm a winner" at all. Suddenly, it was blindingly obvious what she'd been trying to tell me: "I'm Lowenna."

I nodded. I wasn't sure I could trust myself to speak.

Lyle stared at me. His face was so white, I wondered if he was going to be sick. His eyes were dark like the deepest caves in the sea. He held my gaze for . . . I don't know how long. It felt like forever. The room seemed to close around us, keeping everything else on the outside and leaving the three of us alone in this new world that made no sense and that none of us knew how to explore.

Eventually, Lyle spoke. In a voice like gravel, he slowly said, "You'd better tell me everything."

And so, between us, we did. We told him all of it—even the parts that we were nervous about, in case we were in trouble.

"We didn't mean to trespass," Aaron stressed when we told him about finding the chair. "We fell, we got lost, and—"

"It doesn't matter." Lyle brushed aside the interruption. "Go on."

I told him about seeing Lowenna the first time.

"How did she look? How did she seem?" he asked, his voice breaking with urgency.

"She . . ." I hesitated. Should I tell him the truth? That she looked as filled with pain and fear as he did now? "She looked OK," I mumbled eventually.

Lyle let out a breath and his body relaxed a tiny bit. "Oh, thank goodness," he said, and I knew that for once telling a white lie had been the right thing to do.

We told him about going back again; we described the ship, the way it had been almost transparent.

"The weird thing was that only Emily could see Lowenna," Aaron said. "I couldn't see her at all."

"The ship seemed much less real today, too," I added.

Lyle nodded, as if this made some sort of sense to him. "Go on."

"That's about it," I finished off. "We've told you everything."

Lyle didn't respond. He just sat there, leaning forward, his elbows on his knees, his face pulled into a tight frown, his eyes moving from side to side, as if chasing thoughts around his mind.

Then, abruptly, he stood up and turned away from us. Was that it? Now that we'd told him our story, were we being dismissed?

"Are you throwing us out?" Aaron asked.

Lyle spun back around. His gaze was like a dark

tunnel that would trap us forever in its depths if we weren't careful.

"Quite the opposite," he said. "I'm going to take a few deep breaths. Then I'm going to make a hot chocolate for each of us. And then I'm going to come back and sit down and we'll keep talking."

"I . . . I don't know what else there is to say," I blurted out. "We've told you everything."

Lyle nodded slowly. "Yes, I know you have. And believe me, you will *never* know how grateful I am to you for your bravery and your honesty in doing that."

"So what else do you want us to tell you?" Aaron asked.

Lyle paused for a moment. Then in a voice as steady as the horizon, he said, "I don't want you to tell me anything. Now it's my turn. I'm going to tell you *my* story."

Chapter Twelve

*A*aron and I sat together on the sofa, listening to the sounds of Lyle puttering around in the kitchen — a kettle coming to boil, the chink of jars and cups and spoons.

We didn't talk. My mouth was too dry to speak, even if I had a clue of what I might say. I had a hunch that Aaron felt the same.

Instead, we sat in silence and held each other's hands so tightly they could have been our lifelines. Maybe they were.

Eventually, after what felt like ages but was probably less than five minutes, Lyle came back into the room. He handed us our drinks, and I held mine with both hands. My nerves had made my body shiver, and the hot drink warmed me.

"OK," Lyle said. "If you're ready, I'll tell you everything. And when I've done that, between us we'll try to figure out our next move. How does that sound?"

"Perfect," I said. My nerves turned to excitement as Lyle began. While we sipped our hot chocolate, he told us his story—his and Lowenna's story.

"First, some basic facts," Lyle began—which seemed like a good idea. Basic facts sounded safe, solid, known. Until he added, "Let's start with Atlantis."

Aaron's jaw fell open. I nearly dropped my mug.

"Atlantis?" Aaron asked, almost in a whisper.

"Which is a place that exists?" I queried. "As in, like, in actual, real life?"

Lyle nodded. "It's completely secret," he said. "Humans know nothing about it, other than the stories they make up—which are little more than fairy tales."

"What about merfolk?" I asked.

"In the merfolk world, the rumors about Atlantis are *slightly* closer to the truth — but even merpeople are a long way from knowing its full story. Neptune ensures that the secret of Atlantis is the best kept one of all."

"Neptune!" I burst out. "He's in charge of Atlantis?"

Lyle frowned. "Of course," he said. "Neptune is in charge of *everything* having to do with the oceans. Although even he rules from a safe distance."

"So, how do *you* know about it?" I asked.

Lyle turned his dark gaze on me. "Because," he said, "Atlantis is my employer."

"You work for Atlantis?" I gasped. "I thought you were in charge of this island. Is that just a front?" I could feel my hackles rising. Was Lyle going to turn out to be yet another adult who pretended to be one thing just so he could get away with something completely different? I'd met more than enough of those to last a lifetime.

"No, it's not a front. It's part of my job. And it's a very important part. It's just not *quite* as important as the other half."

"Go on," I prompted him.

"OK, so half of my job is the day-to-day running of Fivebays Island and looking after visitors, as you have seen."

I stopped myself from making any comment

about how we hadn't actually seen *that* much of him looking after the island, or its visitors—i.e., us.

"To be fair, most of the work with visitors is Lowenna's job," Lyle added quickly. "My work is mostly in the background."

"So half of your job is looking after the island," Aaron said. "What's the other half? The Atlantis half?"

Lyle's voice was steady. "I am a Record Keeper," he said.

"A *what*?" I asked.

"A Record Keeper—for Atlantis. We keep records of . . . of people. And boats."

"Which people?" Aaron asked. "What boats?"

"Look. What I'm telling you now is absolutely top secret. I could get into serious trouble for sharing this. Do you understand?"

"Of course we do," Aaron and I replied in unison.

"OK. So, I don't know what tales you might have heard about it, but Atlantis is where people and ships go when they are lost at sea. My job is to check them in."

"Check them in?" I asked. "How do you know when they've gone there?"

"Two ways. You've already seen my lookout spot. When I went there yesterday, I could tell that someone had been there. I just didn't know it was you."

"You mean the Watchtower?" Aaron asked. "That wasn't just us. *Everybody* went—"

"Not the Watchtower," Lyle interrupted him. "The other lookout place."

"The chair," I said.

Lyle nodded. "It's an outpost, a . . . well, let's say it's a bit like an embassy."

"For Atlantis?" Aaron asked.

"Yes."

"That's why it's out-of-bounds," I mused.

"And almost impossible to reach without half killing yourself," Aaron added.

"I'd apologize, but, strictly speaking, you weren't supposed to go there."

"We didn't mean to," I mumbled.

Lyle held up a hand. "I know. And you're not being punished. I'm grateful. If you hadn't been there, we wouldn't be having this conversation—and you have given me my first ray of hope in days."

"OK, go on," Aaron said.

"Lookout Reach—the place you found—is where I am based for much of the time," Lyle continued. "I see boats from there—even ones that are not visible to most people, only to certain types."

"Certain types?" I asked.

Lyle paused. Then he said, "I am a semi-mer, like you."

My mouth literally dropped open as I stared at him. "And Lowenna?" I asked.

He nodded. "She was a semi-mer, too." Then he shook his head. "*Is.* Lowenna *is* a semi-mer. I refuse to believe she has gone."

"Go on," I said gently.

"So, I was at my lookout post yesterday, just before we met at Deep Blue Bay."

"Of course! It was you!" I burst out. "I *saw* you." I turned to Aaron. "Remember, when we helped the others who were stuck on the ledge? I saw something in the water. You convinced me that it must be one of our friends from Shiprock. It wasn't— it was Lyle!"

"I've been working overtime," Lyle admitted. "Only, I'm not checking anyone *in* at the moment. I'm trying to learn if I can check them *out*."

"Check them out of Atlantis?" I asked. "Is that possible?"

"Rarely," Lyle replied in a hoarse whisper.

"So, once people go to Atlantis, they never come back?" Aaron asked.

Lyle shook his head. "Only those with specialist knowledge of Atlantis and its ways stand even the smallest chance of making it. And those who know the ways of Atlantis are unlikely to have found themselves there in the first place. So, no, hardly anyone comes back from Atlantis. In any case, most don't want to."

"Why not?" I asked.

Lyle shook his head and half smiled. "It is the

most dazzling place. City walls that shine like gold, staircases that take you to the tops of trees where birds sing the most beautiful tunes, rivers that run with the sweetest drinks, and sunlight that warms you all the way through to your bones."

"It sounds amazing," Aaron said.

"Yes, it does," Lyle answered. "But it is not all that it seems. And it doesn't last."

"So you want to get someone away?" Aaron asked.

I swallowed. "Lowenna," I put in.

Lyle glanced at me and nodded. "Lowenna and I work for Atlantis from this island. I check people in, but she helps keep them from ever getting there in the first place." Lyle paused. "You understand what I'm saying, don't you?"

"I . . ." I hesitated.

"Atlantis is where those at sea go when they are *lost*." He emphasized the last word and waited for us to register what he meant.

"Lost?" I said eventually. "As in . . ."

Lyle nodded slowly. "As in gone. For good. Think of it as a holding place—a last stop between life and death."

I let out a breath.

Before either of us could say anything, Lyle continued. "Lowenna is one of the most highly skilled Way Makers there is."

"Way Maker?" Aaron broke in.

"She guides boats through difficult passages, helps to keep them safe. You already know that this island sits in one of the most dangerous parts of the ocean. Well, unseen by the ships or their passengers, Lowenna swims ahead of them and helps them through channels they don't even know exist. Atlantis has a sort of magnetic pull. The Way Makers use this to make alterations to a ship's course without its occupants even knowing they are doing so. That's what Lowenna did—*does.* She keeps passing boats safe from a journey that no one wants them to make."

"A journey to Atlantis," Aaron finished.

I started to make connections. "Guiding *Prosperous II,*" I muttered. The ship had been due to pass here last Friday. "That was her job, wasn't it?"

Lyle tried to reply. He opened his mouth but nothing came out. So I continued instead.

"Lowenna was supposed to help keep *Prosperous II* and its passengers safe. Am I right?"

Without lifting his head, Lyle nodded. For a moment, no one spoke. What could we say?

Eventually, in a soft croak, Lyle went on. "We had lunch together. The ship was due to pass at four in the afternoon. It's been past before, many times. There has never been a complication. Lowenna went off to work with a smile. I can see her now—her eyes sparkling, her hair ..."

I reached a hand out and touched his arm. Lyle

let my hand rest for a moment, then moved his arm to swipe a hand across his eyes. "She had something to share with me — said she would tell me after work. She was going to make us a special dinner." He paused for ages, before adding hoarsely, "She never came back."

"Oh, no. That's awful," I said.

"Do you know what happened?" Aaron asked.

"I didn't at the time. I watched the ship from Lookout Reach — smiled to myself as I saw it weaving through the channels. I knew Lowenna was steering it along. And then . . ." He stopped.

"And then?" I nudged him.

Lyle shook his head, as if he were trying to deny the truth of his own words. "And then it went," he said finally. "Disappeared. I saw it go."

"Go?" I asked. "How did it go?"

"Straight down. As if it had been sucked under and swallowed up by the sea in one mouthful. All that was left behind was a line of giant bubbles across the surface of the ocean."

Memories of the kraken came into my head — a huge, fierce sea monster that stole treasure and gold from ships that strayed into the Bermuda Triangle. But even the kraken couldn't gobble up a ship of that size in one bite.

"It was an earthquake," Lyle said flatly. "Happened out there in the channel. Two plates under the earth shifting right beneath the boat. Add that to the high tide and the magnetic power from Atlantis that Lowenna was exerting to keep the boat on track, and you have a powerful combination."

"What happened?" asked Aaron.

"In short, the earth opened up beneath the ship, sent a rocket of bubbles and air shooting upward, hit Lowenna's magnetic force, and sucked the boat right out of the sea and down into the vacuum below. Earth, air, water, tides, all mixed together with the ship stuck in the middle. Ten seconds it took—and it was gone. The ship. The people. My wife."

Suddenly, everything made sense. This had all happened on Friday—the day before we'd arrived. No wonder Lyle had been in such a state the whole time we'd been here. A bunch of visiting kids was hardly going to be his priority when his wife had just gone missing.

"Why didn't you say something?" I asked. "Why didn't you cancel our trip?"

Lyle almost laughed. "If I'd had enough spare thoughts in my head to do so, I would have," he admitted. "But all my thoughts were on Lowenna and the ship. I had completely forgotten you were even coming till your teacher called from the beach to say you were here."

"I'm not surprised," Aaron said. "Jeez. We were the last thing you needed."

Lyle hesitated before replying. "Maybe," he said

after a while. "Or maybe you were *exactly* what I needed."

"Really?" I asked. "Why?"

"Look. Here's what I know . . . The ship went missing and the earthquake took Lowenna down with it."

"You know that for sure?" Aaron interrupted. "I mean, there isn't any chance that she just got stuck in the rubble of the earthquake but is out there somewhere now and will be home soon?"

I envied Aaron's innocent hope. He hadn't seen the woman in the porthole. He didn't have the panic in her eyes burned into his mind.

"She went down with the ship," Lyle said. "I know it. I tried to tell myself otherwise at first, but it's been gone for three days and she hasn't returned. She's gone. Even if I had wanted to hope, wanted to tell myself that the ship had simply changed course and Lowenna had stayed out at sea for some reason, I couldn't. See, when a ship and its people are lost at sea, the other place I see them is on my radar in the Watchtower."

"We didn't see a radar," Aaron pointed out.

I remembered the locked door with the PRIVATE! NO ENTRY! sign. I guessed the radar was in there.

"We don't include it on the guided tour," Lyle answered.

We hadn't had much of a guided tour, but I wasn't going to call Lyle out on that right now.

"I avoided going to the Watchtower for hours, telling myself that the ship had just changed its course and Lowenna would be home soon," Lyle went on. "But by nighttime, I knew I had to face the truth, and I went to look. I could see then that the ship had been lost, Lowenna with it, and I had to check them into Atlantis."

"So that was when you gave up?" I asked.

"Well, yes, but only temporarily. Because on Saturday, something extremely unusual happened. Something I have never seen before — not once a ship has been recorded as entering Atlantis."

"You saw it," Aaron said.

"I did. I saw it for the first time late afternoon on Saturday, shortly before you arrived. I was at my lookout point. It was twenty-four hours since the ship had disappeared, and I was waiting there, hoping for . . . I don't know what I was hoping for. I was almost *beyond* hope, but then I saw it! Just for a matter of minutes — but it was there."

"Like when we saw it the next day," I murmured.

"Sunday, yes. I had a lot of catching up to do, organizing your week, so I couldn't get back there again till later in the day."

"Which was when I saw you."

Lyle nodded. "I figured if there was any chance of seeing the ship a second time, it would be on the high tide again, and from the same place — Lookout Reach."

"That was why you said to meet *after* high tide," I concluded, suddenly remembering Lyle joining us with wet hair. He hadn't showered especially for us; he'd been in the ocean! "So you could go back to Lookout Reach to search for the ship first."

"Exactly."

"And did you see it that time?" Aaron asked.

"Clear as anything." Lyle smiled gently, as if seeing his wife in front of him and smiling just for her. "The ship was out there, heading this way. Fifteen minutes, I had, before she was gone again."

"Have you seen it since?" I asked.

"I glimpsed it this morning. But barely. It was fading. She's going from me." His voice broke on the last words.

"Can't you go after it?" Aaron asked. "You work for Atlantis — can't you just go there and bring her back?"

Lyle almost laughed. He shook his head. "Believe me, I would if I could. But Atlantis is not a place you can just go to. It is a place where you find yourself — if you are very unlucky. My job is on *this* side. It is a numbers game. I am more or less an accountant, keeping track of losses and gains."

"So no one can go there," I said. "But how come *we* can see the ship? And why is it fading?"

"I've been asking all the same questions myself, and studying the answers using every bit of knowledge about Atlantis I have," Lyle replied. "I've been up day and night, puzzling over every detail. To my knowledge, this has never happened before in my lifetime. You understand? Never."

"Seeing a ship after it's gone to Atlantis, you mean?" I asked.

"Yes. It's virtually unheard of. I mean, there are rumors. I've read the writings of the old RKs."

Aaron frowned. "RKs?"

"Record Keepers. The ones that went before me. I've been studying their stories, their experiences, to see if I could find anything that would help."

"What did you discover?" I asked.

"Not much. Some wrote of occasional sightings of ships that had returned. Others talked of portals between this world and Atlantis. But it was all conjecture. There was no hard evidence. None of them could prove anything. To be honest, there wasn't much I hadn't heard before, and I've never believed any of it — till now."

"Till you saw the ship with your own eyes," I said.

"Exactly. Since then, I've been unable to think of anything else. The sightings gave me a shred of hope. The fact that you saw it, too, has doubled that hope. But dashed it at the same time."

"Dashed it?" I asked. "Why is that?"

"The sightings meant that those on board the ship were trying to come back — to leave Atlantis."

"But that's a good thing, isn't it?" Aaron insisted.

"That is, yes, but they are fading—which means that the attempts are failing. Each time they try and fail, the chance of a successful return gets slimmer. And each day that goes by takes them farther and farther away. As a Record Keeper, I know that it takes six days from when a ship passes through my radar before it's gone for good."

I sipped my drink. It was almost cold now, but the chocolatey taste was still good. "What do you mean?"

Lyle sighed. "It's complicated."

"Try us," Aaron said.

"Well. Time works differently in Atlantis. When a ship enters, the first day there is the same length as a day here. On day two, it begins to change."

"In what way?" I asked.

"Time passes strangely," Lyle replied. "On the second day, twenty-four hours in this world is like a week in Atlantis. Day three is like a month. Day four is six months. On day five, anything can happen. Time just goes wonky. It could pass like a normal day, or it could be a year—or anything in between. Everything is kind of skewed until day six . . ." His voice faded away and he looked down at the floor.

"What happens on day six?" Aaron asked.

Lyle spoke to the carpet. "At the end of day six, it's over. The ship is gone forever. There have never been *any* tales of a ship returning after day six. Not even rumors."

I counted on my fingers. *Prosperous II* had disappeared on Friday. If that was day one, that meant today was day four.

Lyle must have seen me adding it up. "Yes," he said. "Two more days and then I have to give up hope for good."

"But I *saw* her," I insisted. "I saw the ship, saw Lowenna."

"Fading," Lyle pointed out.

"Yes," I admitted reluctantly. "But still there."

"How come Emily saw Lowenna and I didn't?" Aaron asked. "And why could she see the ship more clearly?"

Lyle shook his head. "I don't know. I still have more questions than I do answers. I know this, though." He looked me hard in the eyes, holding me with his stare. "I could barely see the ship from Lookout Reach today — yet you saw it quite clearly. You have given me hope. I was almost out of that."

I didn't know what to say to that. I couldn't really speak anyway, as something about the look in Lyle's eyes was clogging up my throat.

A moment later, he stood up. "Look, you'd better be going. Your teacher will be wondering where you are, and the last thing we need is for you to get into trouble."

Aaron and I stood up, too. Lyle led us to the door.

"I need to think this through," he said. "I'll spend all night working on it. Will you come and see me again in the morning?"

"Of course," I answered for us both.

"Good. Come before breakfast," Lyle said. "We'll make an early start. I'm not giving up. Not until I have to."

We paused on the doorstep. "We're not giving up, either," I said. "However we can help, we will."

Lyle nodded a thank-you at us both. And then, closing the door softly behind us, he went inside and we headed back to the road. I glanced over my shoulder as we walked away. Lyle was in the window. He gave a brief wave and I waved back.

Aaron put an arm around me as we made our way back to the cabin. We didn't talk. I guessed his thoughts were as dark and as sad as mine. And at the heart of them, just one question: Did we really stand a chance of rescuing a ship from Atlantis before time was up in two days?

Chapter Thirteen

I barely slept on Monday night. When I did, it was accompanied by restless dreams where I was trapped underwater in the darkness, or in an abandoned ship, surrounded by dark, prying eyes, all staring blankly at me.

I woke, sweating and breathless, for the third time in an hour. I checked the clock. Six fifteen. I turned over in my bed. Turned again. Pulled my sheets off, put them back on. Nothing was working.

Finally, I gave up. I got dressed and crept downstairs. The place was silent. Well, of course it was.

Why would anyone else be up and about at six thirty in the morning?

Except—someone was. Not in the house, but outside, across the road. Sitting on a wooden bench in his front garden. I guessed he was having as much trouble sleeping as I was. More, probably.

I quietly opened the front door and went outside. "Lyle," I called as I crossed the road and went over to him.

He glanced up at me, his dark eyes not seeing me for a moment, not recognizing anything. His blank, unseeing look reminded me of the second time I saw Lowenna.

He shook himself. "Emily," he said. "What are you doing up so early?"

I shrugged. "Couldn't sleep."

"Me neither."

"Are you OK?" I asked, then wanted to kick myself. Of course he wasn't OK.

Lyle stood up. "Actually, I'm glad you're here," he said. "I've been up all night working on this, and I think I'm finally getting somewhere." He waved a hand at the bench. "Look, take a seat. I'll just get some coffee and grab my paperwork, and then we can discuss everything—if you're still on board."

"Of course I am! Should I go and wake Aaron?"

Lyle glanced at his watch. "Let's let him sleep a bit longer. We can update him later. Plus, there are a few things I've figured out that I'd like to share with you while Aaron's not here."

As he went off to get the coffee, I couldn't help a shiver from darting through me. I was probably just cold. The sun hadn't even risen yet. But I had the feeling it wasn't just that. What had Lyle figured out? And what on earth did he need to tell me that he didn't want Aaron to hear?

I sipped my coffee, grimacing as I swallowed. I don't think anyone under thirty actually likes coffee at the best of times, and this cupful was so strong, it looked like dirt. At least it was warming me up, though.

Lyle noticed my face. "I can get you a hot chocolate if you prefer."

"No. I'm fine." I didn't want to hold this conversation up any longer, even if the coffee was starting to give me palpitations.

Lyle pulled over a fold-up chair and sat down beside the bench. "OK, so, as you know, we've seen the ship at high tide."

"And low tide, too," I added.

"Yes, at slack tide. You know what that is?"

"When the movement stops in between the tide coming in and going out."

"Correct. So the first thing I've figured out is *why* we've seen it at these times. At first I thought it was just because the ship had gone down at high tide, but after talking to you yesterday, I realized I was wrong. We're seeing it then because these are the times *between*."

"Between?"

"The ship was caught between earth, sea, and air—that's what allowed it to become lost to Atlantis. We see it between the tide coming in and going out."

"And the reason we see it is because we are between human and mer!"

Lyle wagged a finger at me. "Exactly. You're a quick learner."

"So that explains why only Aaron and I could see it when we were there with others, but what about the fact that the ship seems to be fading?"

"OK, that's the next thing." Lyle picked up a notebook he'd brought out with him and flicked through the pages. "Here's what I've come up with. The fact that we're seeing the ship means that it's trying to get back. The fact that it's fading means that those on board are giving up. You remember I told you about time working differently in Atlantis?"

"Uh-huh."

"So, remember, the day it went missing— Friday—was day one. That means it's now day five. In Atlantis, they've been gone for more than six months already. By the end of today, it could be anything up to a year. Even in normal circumstances, that's long enough for at least some of them to start giving up."

"And Atlantis isn't normal."

"Not even *close* to normal. Atlantis has special qualities that make you forget you ever lived anywhere else, make you want to stay there forever. It's like a kind of paradise, and it works like a magnet, keeping you happy and content, smoothing the passage . . . until the six days are up."

"When it's all over and you're never coming back."

"Exactly."

I thought for a moment. "So by the end of tomorrow, that's it, game over?"

Lyle nodded. "That's how it works."

"So what can we do?" I asked. "Are we giving up?"

"No! Never. Not while there's still a chance," he replied with such force he almost sounded angry.

"OK, go on," I said carefully.

Lyle ran a hand through his hair. "OK, so you remember yesterday I told you how some folks believe that there is a portal between the two worlds?"

"You said that was why we were seeing the ship."

"Yes—but this portal isn't just about *seeing* the ship. In some quarters, there are whispered rumors about the possibility of *moving* between the two worlds. No one has any *proof* that this can be done, but there are stories."

"And what do the stories say?"

"It's very rare that this portal can open—and most believe it is only a myth, anyway," Lyle went on. "But if it is true, I think we have a chance."

"That's wonderful!" I said.

He frowned. "Well, yes. I'm going to try it—but I don't know if it will work."

"Why not?"

"OK, this is about being between two states. The ship was pulled down between earth and sea, and it is now stuck between this world and the next. So, it was in two in-between states when it disappeared. Do you realize how significant that is?"

"Umm, I think so."

"Well, the stories say that if you can double the number of between states that took the ship, the boat will appear again, even if it is no longer trying to get back. And then you can find a key to creating a bridge between the two worlds."

"Double the between states? So you mean we need four of them and we can reach the ship?"

"That is what the stories say. And even if they are true, the chances of this being achieved are so slim, it's no wonder that most believe the stories are myths with no foundation. But I'm determined to try. While there's hope, I'm *not* giving up."

"OK, we need four states . . ." I mused. "Well, first, there's us being semi-mers."

"Correct. That's one."

"And then there's the fact that we see the ship at slack tide, when the ocean is between movement in and out."

"That's two. Which is enough to *see* it," Lyle agreed. "We need two more to reach it."

I thought as hard as I could. What else was there? I shook my head. "I can't think of any more."

Lyle flicked through his book and opened it on a page with times and numbers written tightly together in columns.

I leaned in to look. "What's that?" I asked.

"Tide tables." Lyle ran a finger down the page. He stopped at Sunday's date. "Look, see, these were the times of high and low tide on Sunday, and yesterday, too. This is when the ship was visible."

I read the figures. They tallied with when I'd seen it. "OK," I said. "But what—"

"Look here." Lyle pointed at today's date. High tide had passed about half an hour ago. Today's low tide would be at 12:18 p.m. The next high was at 6:20 p.m.

"So that's when we should see it today," I said.

"Yes, if they are still trying to get back. If they haven't given up completely yet. But look—this is the important part." He pointed at the next column. "See the high tides for tomorrow?" he said.

Wednesday's high tides were at 6:41 in the morning, and then at 6:53 in the evening. What was he getting at?

"I still don't see what's so significant," I said.

Lyle flipped over to the next page in his book. More numbers.

"What are these?" I asked.

"Sunrise and sunset times," he said. "It's just after the fall equinox, which means that dawn and dusk are more or less twelve hours apart." He ran his finger down to Wednesday's date. "See that?" he asked. "What time does it say for dawn?"

"6:46 a.m.," I read aloud.

"Exactly. Right in the middle of slack tide! And dusk is at 6:59 p.m., right in the middle of slack tide again!"

My brain cells were working as hard as they could. Finally, I understood what Lyle was saying. "That's another between state! Dawn and dusk are in between day and night!"

Lyle smiled. "Yes!"

"And it's on day six. The last day we could possibly reach the ship," I mused.

"From what I've learned, if we *can* find a fourth between state, and *if* the portal exists, it will open at dawn for the length of the slack tide. On the next high tide, it will mirror this movement and open again, before closing for good."

"That's a lot of ifs," I murmured.

"I know. But ifs are the best thing we've got right now."

"So what's the fourth between state?" I asked.

Lyle shook his head. "I can't think of one." He bit on the end of a fingernail. I hadn't seen him do that before.

"What?" I asked. "There's something you're not saying."

"No, there isn't," he said quickly. "No. I'm not. I can't."

"What? What is it?" I insisted.

Lyle looked as if he might cry. His eyes narrowed into dark holes. "I can't," he said again.

"Please," I begged. "What is it? Tell me."

He paused for ages. Then in a really quiet voice, he said, "It's you."

"What? What's me?"

"You can do things that neither Aaron nor I are capable of. You experienced the ship more strongly than Aaron did. You saw Lowenna when Aaron didn't. More important than that, *she* saw *you*. I wish it were me — and we'll figure something out because I'm not going to let you use it — but, Emily, you have one more between quality."

"Really? What is it?"

Lyle smiled sadly. He looked as if he'd disappeared somewhere miles away. "It wasn't until I watched the two of you walk away last night that I realized what it was."

"What? What is it?"

Lyle held my eyes with his and said, "You are between like and love."

I gawped at him. I don't know what I had been expecting him to say, but it certainly wasn't that. "I'm *what?*"

"I can see it. You're teetering between the two states. You probably won't be for much longer, but you are now."

"But—but—" I spluttered. "I mean . . . what about Aaron? Isn't he the same?"

Lyle paused for a moment, then shook his head. "No," he said simply. "Aaron is not the same."

I wanted to ask him more. At least, half of me did. The other half didn't really want to know. On top of the way Aaron had been responding to some of the things I'd said this week, it was obvious what he meant. Aaron was nowhere *near* loving me, never mind halfway there!

Just then, with perfect timing, I heard someone calling across to us. I looked up. Aaron!

He made his way over the road. "There you are," he said, closing the gate behind himself and joining us in Lyle's garden. "I guess you couldn't sleep, either?"

"Mm," I said. I couldn't speak. I could barely look at him. My cheeks burned as if there were a fire right in front of my face. I was in between like and love? Was I? *Really?* I mean, *could* you even love someone at my age? Especially when it was so obvious that they didn't feel the same way. He did at least *like* me, though, didn't he? I hadn't gotten *that* wrong?

"We were just talking about you." Lyle broke into my thoughts.

"Really? All good, I hope?" Aaron said as he sat down next to me on the bench.

"Mm," I said again. *Seriously?* Was this all I was going to be capable of uttering from now on?

"Just discussing our plan of action," Lyle said, saving me from the need for further explanation. He summarized what he'd told me about the slack tide and the reason the ship was fading. Luckily, he didn't go into any more detail.

"So we have to act quickly," Aaron said.

"Yep," Lyle agreed. "And I've found out what we need to do. I believe that a portal will open early tomorrow morning, on the high tide. It will be our one chance to reach the ship and bring it home."

"I'll do it!" Aaron announced without a second's hesitation.

Lyle laughed softly. "I thought you'd say that," he said. "But no. You can't. I'm going to figure out a way that I can get through it. I'm not letting either of—"

"I'm doing it," I said firmly.

Both of them turned to look at me.

"I'm going," I repeated. As I said it, I got a tingly, wriggly feeling in my stomach, as if a tiny octopus were tickling me with its tentacles. I know I should have been scared, but I was excited, too. I was going to find a mythical portal. I was going to bring Lowenna back. I was going to go to Atlantis!

Aaron held out a hand, as if to stop me from running off to find the ship right then. "No! Emily, it could be dangerous." He glanced at Lyle. "I mean, I think it could be. *Is* it dangerous?"

"Oh, yes," Lyle confirmed. "The dangers are plentiful and varied. The biggest danger of them all is the risk of getting across to the ship but never making it back again."

I swallowed. The tentacles in my stomach tickled harder. "Being lost forever in Atlantis?"

"Yes. That's why I'm not letting you go. I'll think of something. We just need to figure out together how —"

"*I'm* going," I said. "I'm doing it."

"Emily, no!" Aaron said again. "If anyone's doing it, I am."

Lyle stopped him. "Aaron, you can't. Right now, Emily is the only one who could even attempt it."

Aaron glanced between the two of us. "Why?" he asked. "How do you know?"

"Because I saw Lowenna," I blurted out before Lyle had the chance to say anything embarrassing. "Because I saw the ship more clearly. Guys, you know it's true. I'm the best hope of bringing Lowenna home." I looked from Aaron to Lyle. "I'm the *only* hope."

Lyle dropped his head. He knew it was true.

Aaron let out a hard breath. "I'll go with you all the way to the portal," he said. "I'll stay with you till you get across. I'll do everything I can to keep you from danger, OK? That's the deal."

I felt myself melt. I didn't care if he didn't feel the same way as me. At least he wanted to look after me. He was *so* sweet. He made me—wait! He was making my feelings stronger. I couldn't let that happen! What if I stopped being between feelings? What if his being so nice tipped the scales from like into love?

"Aaron, don't be so sappy!" I snapped, my words not reflecting my feelings at all. "I'll be fine."

Lyle caught my eye. He knew what I was doing. "Emily, if you're absolutely determined . . ."

"I am."

"Well, then, we'll all do everything we can to keep you from harm," he said. "But you need to think carefully about this. I can't ask it of you. I won't. It's not right for—"

"You're *not* asking it of me," I interrupted. "I'm *telling* you: I'm doing it. I want to. I need to." I wasn't going to spell it out for Lyle, but I had to do this for myself almost as much as for him. It wasn't only that I seemed to be completely incapable of resisting an adventure; it also felt like the only way I was ever going to get Lowenna's desperate face out of my mind.

Lyle swallowed hard. His Adam's apple bobbed

up and down a couple of times before he spoke again. "Thank you," he said hoarsely. He reached awkwardly for my hand and squeezed it.

I didn't know what to say. I wasn't sure I'd be able to speak anyway, so it didn't really matter. A moment later, Lyle checked his watch and stood up. "It's almost breakfast time," he said. "You'd better get going."

"Shall we meet you later?" Aaron asked.

"Yes." He pulled a piece of paper out of his back pocket and unfolded it. "You've got Races and Relays with Shiprock this morning and Knowledge and Nets at the harbor this afternoon. How about you hang around at Harbor Bay after that? I'll tell your teacher I've got a special assignment for you that only semi-mers can do."

"Which isn't really very far from the truth," I pointed out.

"Look, are you sure about this? I don't want—"

"Please," I said, stopping him. "You couldn't keep me from doing this, even if you tried," I said. "We'll be fine. All of us. I'm going to bring Lowenna home."

"We'll see you later," Aaron said.

Lyle waved as we got up. "Thank you again," he whispered.

I smiled. "No problem."

And with that, we turned away and headed back across the road to join the others for breakfast.

Aaron's fingers found mine, and I held his hand tightly.

"How do you feel?" he asked.

"Fine. Honestly, I'm cool," I said.

I wasn't going to let him see it or he'd try to stop me, but the thought of what lay ahead was turning my insides to jelly. I mean, of course, I could hardly wait to get going. Magical adventures were pretty much my favorite things. But if I thought about it too much—which I was trying not to do—it *was* kind of ridiculously scary, and dangerous, as well.

"Wonder what's for breakfast," Aaron said. "My tummy's rumbling!"

"Yeah, mine too," I said. And it was true. My stomach was turning around in so many circles it felt like a tangled, knotted fishing net.

But it had nothing to do with being hungry.

Chapter Fourteen

*H*ey, what do you think of this?" Mandy lifted the net she'd been working on and put it over her head. "It's my new shower cap. How does it look?"

I laughed. "I don't think you'll be starting a new fashion trend." I held mine out in front of me. "What about mine? I'm thinking I could use it as a bag."

Mandy studied my netting. "As long as you don't mind losing everything you put in it," she said, placing her arm through one of the holes.

"OK, so maybe we're not the best net makers in the world," I admitted.

Aaron and I had told Mandy and Shona everything earlier, and it was good to laugh and do something different. Take my mind off things for a bit.

"OK, eighth-graders," Miss Platt called as she looked around at our dismal efforts, "I think we've all learned about as much as we are ever going to learn about making fishing nets." She turned to Lyle, who was helping Tom and Maggie finish up their net. "Lyle, I think it's safe to say there won't be too much competition in the net-making industry for the time being."

Lyle stood up and smiled as he looked around at us. "You've all done a great job," he said.

"Now, then, how about some volunteers to help put things away?" Miss Platt asked.

A couple of girls put their hands up. Miss Platt nodded at them. "Evie and Amanda, thank you. Could you fetch the boxes from the top of the beach and help put all the nets back in, please? Grab a friend each to help take the boxes back up to the house."

Lyle looked around the group. "I could do with some more volunteers to help me attach some ropes back onto the jetties." He looked over at me and made a *This-is-where-you-volunteer* kind of face at me. "Maybe a couple of good swimmers . . ."

"I'll do it!" I burst out before anyone else could.

Aaron quickly stuck his hand in the air. "I'll help."

"Great." Lyle beckoned us over. "The rest of you can head back with Miss Platt. Hope you've had a good afternoon."

"They've had a lovely afternoon," Miss Platt replied. "What do we say, children?"

As the class shouted thank-yous to Lyle, Aaron and I made our way to the end of the jetty. We waited for the others to leave with the nets and boxes. Once they were gone, Lyle came over.

"All right," he said. "Let me tell you the plan."

Aaron and I huddled in close as Lyle spoke. "I've done some more research," he said. "I've come up with three reasons a ship might not be able to escape Atlantis—even if any of its crew or passengers know the route, as Lowenna does. The chances of it happening *at all* are so remote as to be almost nonexistent. But the fact that Lowenna is a skilled navigator and that we've seen the ship, makes me think that there is a tiny possibility that they are trying."

"Go on," Aaron said. "What are the three reasons?"

"One, they're already dead and it's too late."

His words made my insides jump like a flying fish. Before I could say anything, he went on. "But it can't be that, or we wouldn't have seen the ship at all."

"OK, what are the others?" I asked.

"Two is that they're still alive, but there's something wrong with the ship that's preventing it from coming back."

"The torn sails!" I said. "Could that be it?"

Lyle shook his head. "It's not quite enough. That might be part of it, but it would have to be something to do with the engineering of the ship — something that makes it impossible to drive at all, let alone navigate the treacherous path back from Atlantis. If it is this one, they've got one more day to fix it."

"So, what's the third?" Aaron asked.

"Trying to take something of Atlantis with you."

"What kind of thing?" I asked.

Lyle shrugged. "I don't know. Could be a memento of some sort. It might even be something that's been picked up in Atlantis and brought onto the boat by accident. Remember, once you are there, you are surrounded by so much magic and beauty, you can't imagine ever wanting to be anywhere else. There would be many things you'd want to keep. Whatever it is, if it comes from Atlantis, the ship won't be able to leave while it's on board."

"OK. So it's most likely to be either option two or three that we're talking about," Aaron said.

"I would think so. I hope so, anyway, with all my heart." Lyle turned to me. "But even if it is one of these, your job is extremely hard. If there is something wrong with the ship, you are unlikely to be much help—not unless you have a degree in mechanical engineering that we don't know about!"

I laughed. "No. But at least I'd be able to let them know their time is running out and that they have to hurry. And if it's the third, I can get them to search the ship and return anything that came from Atlantis. Either way, one thing we know for sure is that they stand a better chance of getting away *with* me than if I don't even try."

"It's a small window," Lyle said. "You'll have just over twelve hours. You should be able to come back on the ship with them. There won't be any problem with that. But if not, there is always the portal, when it opens again at dusk. Dusk is also the ship's last chance to escape. Emily are you sure you—?"

"I'm doing it," I said firmly. "What time do I go?"

Lyle's face was a mixture of gratitude and sadness. "I'll meet you early tomorrow. If we get together at six in the morning at Deep Blue Bay, that'll leave enough time to give you any final instructions before the slack tide."

"Sounds good," I said, trying to keep my voice steady so that neither of them would hear my nerves jangling around like broken shells on a rolling wave.

"I found out some more about the portal, too," Lyle went on. "About its location."

"Tell me more."

"There is disagreement on exactly how to find it, but it seems that there are two possibilities. The first is that it's in the spot where the ship disappeared into the ground. We have to hope that those who support this theory are wrong."

"Why's that?"

"Because that would be virtually impossible to find. The portal will open for only a matter of minutes. Nowhere near long enough for you to burrow into the sand—even if you could find the exact spot that opened up to suck the ship through."

"So what's the other theory?" Aaron asked.

"That the ship has a weak point."

"A weak point?" I repeated. "You mean, like, in its construction or something?"

Lyle shook his head. "A different kind of weak point. Those who argue this theory say that there will be one point on the ship where the connection is strongest. The place where your vision was clearest."

As Lyle spoke, I had no doubt where this point would be. The spot I'd seen in my mind ever since I'd been there. The spot where I'd almost felt as if I could reach through and be inside the ship myself: the porthole where I'd seen Lowenna.

Lyle had no need to explain further. "Those people are right," I said.

He nodded. He knew what I was talking

about—*where* I was talking about. "Yes," he said. "I understand."

"Where?" Aaron asked.

"The porthole."

"Yes, I know you mean the portal. But where are you saying it is?"

"I didn't say portal," I insisted. "I said *porthole*. The porthole *is* the portal."

"Oh." Aaron frowned. "That's weird."

"Yeah."

Before Aaron and I got too carried away with the difference between portholes and portals, Lyle went on. "There are two more things." He dug around in his pocket and pulled out some folded sheets of paper. "I managed to get the passenger list," he said as he opened out the sheets and flattened them on his knee.

"Wow, how did you do that?" Aaron asked.

"I have all sorts of contacts in my line of work," Lyle replied lightly. Then he passed me the papers. They were a random mix of photos and text. "There were six members of crew and twelve passengers," he went on. "I've got photos of them all for you. Try to memorize their faces before you go. It'll help you to find them more quickly once you get there."

If I get there.

"There are way more photos than that," Aaron said.

"I know. The rest are of their families."

178

"Why do I need photos of their families?" I asked.

"You don't. *They* do. The photos will help them to remember."

"Remember their families?" Aaron asked. "Surely they won't have forgotten them in five days?"

"It's not five days for them. It's already been six months," Lyle reminded him. "And by the time Emily gets to them, it will be even more than that. And it's not just about the length of time. It's about the magic that Atlantis exerts. It makes you forget. It forces thoughts of your old life out of your mind. Makes you believe that Atlantis is all you want, all you've ever known."

"So the photos are to remind them of their old lives," I said.

"Their *real* lives," Lyle corrected me. "You can tell them all you like, but they won't believe you until they feel it for themselves. It has to be something that they can hold or see. The photos are *essential*." He reached into his pocket again. This time he brought out a mini snow globe.

He passed the globe to me. The flakes twinkled and fell as he held it out. As they landed, I could see why he'd given it to me. Inside it was a photo. The same as the one in Lyle's house. Lowenna and him together, smiling on their wedding day.

I took the snow globe from him. He didn't need to explain what that was for.

"Lowenna will remember you," Aaron said.

I thought about her eyes, her desperation. "She *does* remember you," I added.

Before Lyle could reply, we heard shouting behind us and all turned to look. Some of the kids from Brightport were coming back down to the harbor. "We'd better be getting back," Aaron said.

Lyle stopped us. "Emily, one final thing. You must remember that you are not immune to the powers and magic of Atlantis. Although you'll be there for only twelve hours, even that will be long enough for you to start forgetting why you are there, or even where you have come from. You will start to forget almost as soon as you arrive. You have to stay strong."

At that, Aaron pulled up his sleeve and started fiddling with a chain on his wrist. I'd seen it before. He'd told me his dad had given it to him before he died. Aaron took it off.

"Hold out your arm," he said to me. As I did, he closed the chain around my wrist and shut the clasp firmly. "This will remind you of me, and of home," he said.

Stop being so nice. Stop. Don't. You'll make me—

"OK. You'd better go." Lyle broke into my thoughts. "Go and join the others. Looks like it's free time."

I glanced behind me to see my classmates running down to the water's edge in shorts and T-shirts.

For a brief second, I envied their innocence, their ignorance of all this.

"What will we tell Miss Platt tomorrow?" Aaron asked.

"Just say I'm spending the day with Shiprock," I suggested.

"I don't want to lie to your teachers," Lyle said.

"Then don't," Aaron suggested. "I will. Mandy and I will work it out."

Lyle held his hands up in a mini surrender. "OK. Look, I'll leave that side of it to you. I just—"

"It's covered," I said firmly before he tried to talk me out of it again. We started heading back up the beach. "See you tomorrow," I said to Lyle as we parted company at the top.

"I can't thank you enough," Lyle replied. And with that, he turned away. A moment later, he was gone.

We watched him walk away. "Come on," Aaron said. "Let's join the rest of the class and pretend for a bit that none of this is happening. What do you say?"

As I looked over, I could see Mandy had come down with the others. She waved over at us. Maybe we could go and get Shona, too. The four of us could hang out and play in the water for a while, before the sun set. An evening of fun and hanging out with my friends. Of forgetting about ships and lost people and Atlantis and—all of it.

"I think that sounds like a plan," I said, taking off my shoes and starting to run. "Race you!"

It's amazing how quickly six o'clock in the morning can come. Once we'd filled Mandy and Shona in on everything, Aaron and I spent all evening with them, playing in the water, chasing and racing and diving and laughing together. The others laughed and smiled a lot. I did the same, but on the inside, I was busy wondering if this was the last evening I would ever have like this. Not just with them—with everyone. I thought about Mom and Dad. As far as they were concerned, I was on a nice little geography field trip. What if I never came home? What if I never saw them again? What if—?

No! I couldn't think like that. If I did, I would never go. And I had to. I owed it to all the people stuck in Atlantis on *Prosperous II*. I'd spent all night reading about them and trying to memorize their faces. And now, after a few restless hours' sleep, it was Wednesday morning and we were heading down to the ocean in the semidarkness.

"Hey. Stop it," Aaron scolded me.

"What?"

"Thinking. I can hear you, you know."

"You can . . . ?"

Aaron slung an arm over my shoulder. "Relax, I don't mean literally. I just mean I can *imagine* what you're thinking. You're going to be great. Everything will be fine."

"Hey, guys!" Mandy was running down the road toward us. I pulled away from Aaron.

"What are you doing? It's really early!" I said as Mandy caught up to us.

"I've come to wish you good luck." She shifted from foot to foot. "Take care of yourself," she said. "I'll be so mad at you if you don't come back!"

I pulled her toward me for a hug. "Thanks, Mandy. Hey, I'll be back before you know it."

She hugged me back for a second, then drew away. "You'd better be, fish girl. The rest of this week will be awful if I haven't got my best friend with me." Mandy stopped. "I mean, I didn't mean . . ." she stammered. "I know you've got other best friends. I just meant—"

I stopped her. "I know," I said. "You're one of my best friends, too."

Mandy made a weird scowl, which I guessed was an attempt to hide a smile. "Cool. OK," she said, shoving her hands in her pockets. "I'll let you go. See you tonight, huh?"

"You bet," I told her.

Aaron and I walked down to Deep Blue Bay in silence. There weren't many words that could fill the big question mark we were walking into.

Lyle was already there. So was Shona, her tail flipping nervously from side to side so much that she was almost dancing on the surface of the water.

"I wasn't going to let you go do something this dangerous without coming to see you off," she said.

We dropped into the water to join her. As my legs fizzled and tingled and my tail formed, I glanced at Lyle. His body had done the same thing. It was weird seeing him as a merman. It reminded me how little we knew about him, about this place, about any of this. A fleeting dart of fear stabbed through my body. *What was I doing?*

"Last chance to change your mind," Lyle said as if I'd uttered my thoughts out loud.

I pictured Lowenna. Pictured the ship. And even though it made me feel a little guilty to think it, I realized I was excited about my adventure. Terrified, yes, that, too, of course, but I couldn't help it that part of me was buzzing with adrenaline at the thought of visiting such a magical and mysterious place as Atlantis.

"I'm not changing my mind," I said firmly.

Lyle nodded. "You've got everything?"

"Yes," I said. I had the papers and the snow globe Lyle had given me in one of Miss Platt's waterproof bags.

"And you've got my chain?" Aaron checked.

I held up my wrist to show him that, too.

"OK, let's go," said Lyle. "I'll swim out to the edge of the bay with you."

We swam away from the island together. Out of the bay, out toward the channel, toward the slack tide, the dawn, the ship.

Toward Atlantis.

Chapter Fifteen

We were in the channel, the same place I'd seen the ship before. I checked my watch: 6:35 a.m. We had six minutes till high tide.

"Good luck, Emily," Lyle said. "You will *never* know how grateful I am to you for this."

I nodded a reply to him. I didn't try to say anything.

Then Shona pulled me into a hug. "Please, please be careful," she said.

" 'Course I will," I assured her.

"If anyone can do this, you can. Just get the job done, and come home—safely."

"I will. I promise," I said, wishing I could believe the words as firmly as I said them.

As she let go of me, she started fiddling with a starfish brooch pinned on her top. "Here, take this," she said, unclipping it and holding it out to me.

"What's that for?" I asked, taking the brooch from her.

"It's a backup. In case anything happens to Aaron's chain," she said. "Pin it on your clothes somewhere you can easily see it."

I pinned the starfish on my top, near my shoulder, and fastened it tight. "Thank you," I said, giving her one last hug.

"Thank *you*," she said, "for being so swishy. You make me proud to be your best friend."

Shona let go of me and joined Lyle as Aaron came over. He didn't say anything, just opened his arms. I swam into them and he held me tightly — so tightly I wanted to stay there forever and not do any of this.

Aaron pulled away and held both of my hands in his. "Good luck," he said. "I'll be thinking about you every second."

"Me too," I said.

"No! Don't think about me. Think about what you're there to do. And take care of yourself. If anything happens to you—"

"Nothing's going to happen to me," I said. "I'll be fine."

Aaron lifted my hand, the one with his chain on it, and kissed it.

Stop it! Stop it! You're being too nice!

I pulled away from Aaron so sharply that he jumped back. "What?" he asked.

"I just . . ." I glanced at my watch again: 6:39 a.m. Nearly time. "I have to go. The ship is going to be here in two minutes."

With that, before anyone had the chance to say anything else — or *feel* anything else — I flicked my tail, spun around, and headed toward the exact spot I'd been in when I'd seen the ship with Shona.

6:41 a.m. The movement of the sea slowed to a halt. Fish stopped swimming. The channel seemed to darken as everything stilled.

But no ship.

6:42 a.m.

"Can you see anything?" Shona asked.

"Not yet." I turned to Aaron. "Aaron? Can you see it?"

He shook his head. "It's not here."

6:43 a.m. Three minutes to dawn, when the portal would open. But if there was no ship, there'd be no portal, either.

Were we too late? Had the ship gone for good?

"Wait!" I could just about see something. A faint shimmer. An outline. The ship — it was here! "Can you see it?" I cried.

"No!" Aaron replied. Of course he couldn't. Lyle

had said that if they were no longer trying to get back, the ship would now be visible only if you had four between states—which meant I'd be the only one who could see it.

"Can *you* see it?" Aaron asked.

The ship was growing more visible. It still looked more like a hologram than anything real, but it was there, and it was getting stronger with every passing second. "Just barely," I said.

6:44 a.m. Two minutes to go. A hundred panicked thoughts came into my head. What if I couldn't find the portal? What if I got stuck going through? What if I couldn't get back? What if I never saw Aaron again?

That final thought was like an electric shock to my brain, reminding me of what I had to do. The last thing I could afford right now was to think thoughts like that. It was dangerous; it could make me feel things that I mustn't feel. Not yet. I had to stay *between*. I had to stay focused.

"I'm going to go to Lowenna's window," I said. "I need to be ready when the portal opens."

"I'll swim with you," Aaron replied.

"I'll be praying and wishing and sending you every bit of luck in the world," Lyle added.

"Emily . . ." Shona's voice was muffled. "I don't know if you can still hear me, but if you can, good luck! I know you'll do a swishy job!"

I laughed to myself. Swishy. Only Shona could

describe something like this as *swishy*. She could always make me smile. I looked around me. I could barely see her, but I knew she was there.

"Thank you!" I called back into the silent stillness of the ocean.

Aaron was beside me. "Come on," he said. "We need to go."

One behind the other, we made our way along the channel. As we swam, the ship came and went, fading practically to a see-through image, then returning almost as strongly as the last time I'd seen it.

"Can you still not see it?" I called back to Aaron.

"No. But it doesn't matter. All that matters is that you can."

We were running out of time. My link with the ship was weakening by the second, and the portal still wasn't open. I checked my watch as we swam alongside the ship's hull: 6:45 a.m. One more minute.

We passed window after window. At each one, I glanced into the blackness within as I swam by.

And then we were there, halfway along the ship's hull: the porthole where I'd seen Lowenna. I stopped swimming and peered into the darkness. Nothing. I checked around the porthole frame. I'd noticed a bit of scuffed paint just above the glass last time I was here. Yes, it was still there. This was definitely the right one.

"It's 6:46," Aaron said. "Are you ready?"

My heart thumped like a ship's engine. "I think so."

We waited. The sea was so still, it felt like air. The darkness on the other side of the glass was so black, it looked like night. The ship was weakening by the second.

"What do I do?" I asked. "How do I make the portal appear?"

"I don't know. Maybe—" Aaron began.

"Wait." I stopped him. Something was changing. Above us, I saw a faint twinkle of light. Dawn was breaking. The sun was rising. And then I saw it: the window, the porthole—the portal.

"It's here," I whispered. The glass was shimmering and shining. First a deep purple, then blue, then mauve, pink, yellow, green—the porthole was exploding with color. It was as if a firework display were going on behind it.

"You need to go," Aaron said. "Before it's too late. We don't know how long you've got."

He was right. I flicked my tail and slithered over to the porthole.

As I swam toward the colors, my fear disappeared. As the glass in the porthole melted away, so did my worries. All that was there was color, light, and a space just large enough to swim through. Not only that, but it was a space I *wanted* to swim through. It was as if I craved it, as if I *needed* it. It reminded me of the first time I'd gone into the water during the school swimming lesson; it was that same sensation of being lured by something that scared me but something I couldn't resist.

I stopped in front of the porthole.

"Good luck, Emily," I heard faintly, and I turned to say good-bye to Aaron, but he was already starting to vanish.

"I'll see you soon," I called back. And then I turned to the ship and swam right up to the porthole. A moment's hesitation, and I swam into the colors, into the light, through the porthole that was now a portal.

As I swam, my body felt as if it were moving through an electric current. Every nerve ending jangled and danced and fizzed and sparked with energy. It was almost enough to make me stop and turn back. Almost pain. But then I remembered why I was doing this, and I swam on.

The feeling grew stronger. The lights that had looked so inviting seemed to have turned into a monstrous kind of energy; it felt as if they were attacking me: biting my skin, snapping at my tail, scratching my face.

No! I couldn't do it! I couldn't even remember *why* I was doing it. The sensation was too much; I couldn't bear it.

I tried to turn back, but there was no space. The porthole had become a capsule, with me and the vicious lights battling and squirming inside it.

"Help!" I screamed. "I want to get out!" But there was no one to hear me.

I pushed and kicked with my tail, lashed out with my arms. The lights spun me around, beat me against the sides of the capsule, flung me inside out, as if I were caught in the spin cycle of a washing machine.

No. No. No! I couldn't take it anymore. I didn't have any fight left. I wasn't going to get through.

And then I remembered what I was there for.

I wasn't doing this for fun — and I wasn't doing it for myself. I was doing it for Lyle and for Lowenna.

The thought of her frightened eyes and Lyle's sad face spurred me on. I gathered all the strength I had, visualized my tail turning into a propeller and my arms into the strongest fins in the world, and gave it one last push.

Something changed. Gradually, the energy began to feel a little less hostile. The lights dimmed a tiny bit. It was all I needed to encourage me. I swam as hard as I could, working my arms like a windmill.

And then — when I was on the verge of giving up out of sheer exhaustion — the tingling feeling in my body faded. The colors calmed to soft pastel shades. My tail stopped feeling as if it were under attack from a hundred biting sharks. The lights dimmed to a warm glow and then disappeared completely. I was through. I was inside the ship.

I was in darkness.

I turned back to face the way I'd come in. The shimmering colors had gone, as if it they'd never existed. All I could see was an ordinary porthole. The same one through which I'd seen Lowenna.

Only this time, I was on the inside.

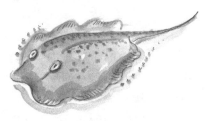

Chapter Sixteen

I guess you could sum up my feelings at that point in two words: sheer panic.

I mean, what else could I logically feel? I had just swum through a window that wasn't a window, through something that felt like a live meteor shower, into a cabin that was in complete darkness, on a ship that kind of existed but not in the traditional sense of the word *exist,* and I was now completely alone with the possibility that I might be stuck here forever.

Sheer panic felt like a supremely sensible thing to feel.

Treading water in the dark, I pulled my thoughts into line. I didn't have long and couldn't afford to waste any time.

I pulled up my sleeve and set a countdown timer on my watch. I had twelve hours. Then I realized something. Even though I was treading water, the cabin wasn't completely underwater. I swam upward, poked my head out, and shook the water out of my hair. The cabin was half submerged and lying on a tilt.

How was it only half underwater when Aaron and I had been swimming way down in the sea to get to it?

I had the feeling this was only the first of many questions I would be asking myself over the next twelve hours.

Pulling down my sleeve, I tried to steady my thoughts. On an impulse, I pulled up my other sleeve. Aaron's chain. I touched it, tracing the delicate links with my fingers.

The chain would keep me safe, remind me what I was here to do — and what I was going back to.

I checked the timer on my watch: 11:57. Three minutes had already passed. It was time to get going.

I flicked my tail and silently glided across the dark cabin and toward the door, which led me out into a long corridor. I swam quickly along the passageway and soon came to a hallway.

Stairs led up and down. Which way?

I swam to a picture on the wall. It was a map of the ship. A YOU ARE HERE arrow pointed to a spot in the middle of the ship. Deck three. There were two decks below me and two above. According to the picture, I was on the deck with the passenger cabins. The one below me had the crew's quarters and a reception area. Below that was a deck for the ship's engines and cargo.

The level above me housed a dining room, a shop, and a panoramic lounge. Above that was the captain's quarters at the front — and the shiny deck where I had seen people walking around at the back.

I swam halfway up the staircase, which was as high as the water went. I sat on a step and waited for my tail to stop flapping, stop tingling, and return to legs. Then, as quietly and as steadily as I could, given that the whole ship was on a steep slope, I gripped the handrail and climbed the staircase to the fourth deck.

I made my way along the corridor toward the small shop. "Hello?" I stepped gingerly into the shop and looked around. Empty.

One wall was lined with shelves full of key chains and coasters with a picture of the ship and the words

Prosperous II on the side. They had all slipped to the ends of the shelves, which were sloping downward with the ship's tilt.

The shop had the feel of a place that had been trashed and then completely forgotten about. Behind the counter, pencils and a bowl of magnets lay on the floor. A rack held T-shirts that had all slipped down to one end.

I made my way to the dining room.

Tables were strewn with forgotten plates and bowls. Coffee machines had unwashed cups and saucers beside them. I picked up one of the cups. Something that looked like cotton balls appeared to be growing in the bottom of it.

The place was completely abandoned. Where *was* everyone?

A door behind the coffee machine was half open. I approached it cautiously. Pushing through the door, I called out again. "Hello? Anyone around?"

This was starting to get creepy.

OK, it was way beyond *starting* to get creepy. It was full-on, out-and-out, brain-mashingly spooky. What had happened to Lowenna? To all of the passengers and crew?

I checked the lounge at the front. Same thing. Completely empty. Corridors: empty. Reception area: deserted. The ship was a ghost town.

Finally, I climbed up to the top deck. I pushed open a heavy glass door and went outside.

The first thing to hit me was the feeling of the air against my skin: warm, soothing, gentle, it was like . . . like what? I'd never felt anything like it before. As smooth as melted caramel, as warm as a summer's day, as comforting as a blanket—it instantly soothed my worries.

There was no one out here, either, but I no longer minded all that much.

In fact, I was struggling to remember whom I was looking for.

Ahead of me, there was a wooden changing hut and a small pool. It looked like a hot tub, although the water was still and had a layer of light-green slime around the edges. Like everything else, it had clearly been neglected for months.

I slid along the downward-sloping deck to the edge of the ship and a couple of deck chairs. I opened the nearest one out into full recline and sat on it. I could just lie here and enjoy the heat and the lovely feeling.

The sun was so warm, so beautiful. I had never felt so at peace, so calm, so happy. I could stay here forever.

I lay down, rolled up my sleeves to enjoy the sunshine, and . . .

Wait! What was that on my arm? The chain! From Aaron. My boyfriend.

I sat right up. What was I even thinking? I wasn't here to sunbathe! I was here to find Lowenna and all the others. How had I let myself forget? Was Atlantis working its magic on me already?

I got out of the chair and clung to the railings, looking out. All I could see was blue. The bluest blue I'd ever seen. The clearest sky, stretching down toward the ocean and blending with it so seamlessly it was hard to tell where the sky ended and the sea began.

I turned away and climbed up the sloping boards to the opposite deck. For a moment, the sun blinded me. It was so bright, I had to shield my eyes. Using my hands as a visor, I eventually managed to see what lay ahead.

A beautiful, sparkling, shimmering blue bay. Behind it, an island. A palm-fringed beach in front of me that looked like a postcard from the world's most exclusive paradise. Behind that, bridges, streams, a waterfall running down to a river beside the beach, sparkling as if it were filled with a million silver coins. Beyond that, buildings that seemed to climb up and down hills all across the island. Houses in a hundred different pastel colors, on hills so green they looked as if they'd been colored in with the brightest felt-tip markers in the world.

I swallowed as I stared across at the island. Suddenly, all I wanted was to get there, to be there, be part of it. I couldn't wait to explore every inch.

And that was when I knew for sure that I wasn't looking at just any old island.

I was looking at Atlantis.

I slipped down to the lower side of the ship and dived into the blue sea. Swimming around the ship, I made my way toward Atlantis.

The sea was turquoise and so clear that the ocean floor looked as if it were in high-definition. Close up, the sand on the beach looked as soft and white as powdered sugar. A single palm tree reached out from each end of the beach, almost horizontally, as if each tree wanted to dip its leaves in the ocean.

A long jetty stretched out from the soft white beach, right into the sea. I pulled myself out of the water and sat on the end of the jetty, shaking myself dry and watching as my tail slipped gradually away and my legs returned.

As I walked up the jetty toward the beach, two people padded over to greet me. A man and a woman, one on either side of the jetty; they wore identical garlands of multicolored flowers around their necks, and they beamed with identical smiles.

"Welcome!" the woman said, reaching out to hug me tightly, as if I were a long-lost friend.

The man handed me his garland. "We are so pleased to have you join us," he said, placing the flowers over my head. "We hope you have a delightful stay. Make yourself at home. Enjoy."

The woman took my hand, and both of them walked across the sand with me. My feet melted into it. It was like walking on marshmallows.

The woman stopped and reached down to a basket in the sand. Where had that come from?

She held it out to me. "Here," she said. "Help yourself."

I stared into the basket. It was full of pink and white marshmallows! Whoa! How had that happened?

I looked at the woman. "Go on," she said, and laughed. "They're for you."

I dug my hand into the basket and pulled out a handful. As I tasted them, I almost fainted from pleasure. They were the sweetest, softest things I had ever eaten in my life.

"Thank you!" I mumbled, my mouth half full of marshmallow.

She laughed again. Then she pointed away from the beach. "See that bridge in front of you? Take it into the city," she said. "You will find much to enjoy. If you have any questions, there are plenty of people around to help you find answers."

The bridge led across a river that ran with the clearest water I'd ever seen. As the water flowed, it twinkled in the sunlight, looking as if it were sprinkled with diamonds.

"Thank you!" I said. I couldn't wait to go and explore.

The man was rummaging around in another basket. "Here," he said. "A welcome gift."

"You've already given me a garland and a basket of marshmallows!" I laughed. I *loved* these people!

The man waved off my reply. "A *real* gift," he said, pulling out a bracelet from the basket. A line of tiny bright diamonds, linked by the most delicate gold chain I'd ever seen.

"Like it?" he asked.

"I love it!" I gasped. It was the prettiest thing I'd ever seen in my life. I wanted to wear it always, show it to ... to whom? I couldn't think of anyone I'd show it to. Couldn't remember anyone's names.

Hold on! I'd show it to all the people I met on this beautiful island! I would get a feathery top just like the woman was wearing, and wear my beautiful new bracelet. I'd smile and laugh and dance and live here forever, the happiest girl alive!

"Hold your hand out," the man said, undoing the clasp.

I held out my arm. No, wait. Not that one. I had a watch on it.

I pulled up my other sleeve, held out my arm—
And saw Aaron's chain.

No! It had happened again! I'd forgotten where I was, what I was here for.

I glanced at the man and woman, both still beaming at me. Didn't they know where they were, where *we* were, *what this place was*?

I pulled down my sleeve again. "Actually, I . . .

er, I think I'll have a little look around first," I stammered. "See what else there is before I choose what to buy."

The woman laughed out loud. "We're not selling, dear," she said. "There are no shops here, only gifts."

I swallowed. "I—I'll just take a walk first, if that's OK," I mumbled.

The man put the bracelet into my palm and closed my fingers over it. "Take it anyway," he said. "All we want is to make you happy."

I took the bracelet and fastened it on next to my watch. "OK. Thank you," I muttered. It *was* beautiful. I supposed there was no harm in keeping it.

The woman touched my arm. Her hand was gentle and soft. It calmed my heart rate down a little. "Don't worry," she said. "You'll be fine. We'll look after you."

I tried to smile at her, but my mouth felt frozen on my face as if it might crack and splinter into pieces.

"OK, thanks," I stammered eventually, and then I made my way toward the bridge.

I could see people on the other side of it—maybe the people I'd come to find. I had to reach them. I had to keep on remembering why I was here.

I checked my timer: 11:08. I had just over eleven hours left. It was time I stepped it up a gear. Nearly an hour had passed already and I had barely started.

As I crossed the bridge, I scanned the other side.

A narrow cobblestone street lined with multicolored buildings ran up a hill and disappeared around a corner. Every building was a different color and shape. Pastel pink next to vivid yellow. Thin tall turrets beside round houses with chimneys — they were so quirky and cute; they reminded me of pictures in a children's storybook.

I stepped off the bridge and onto the cobblestones. As I did, I heard someone begin to sing a tune. It was beautiful, haunting. It made me want to cry and laugh at the same time. I stopped walking and looked around.

The singing stopped.

Huh? Where had it come from? Where had it gone? There were a few people in the street, walking along casually in groups of two or three, smiling and chatting with one another. No one was singing.

I shook my head and continued walking. As I did, the song began again. Which was when I realized — it was coming from the cobblestones! As I walked, the ground shone with soft lights and played its music.

The ground was singing to me?

I quickly brought my wrist to my face. Aaron's chain. *Look at it!* I had to remember why I was here before I got lost in the magic again.

Back on track, I continued walking, scanning

the faces of everyone I passed. I didn't recognize anyone yet.

I followed the cobblestone street around a corner. In front of me, a sky-blue gate led to another road. The gate smelled of fresh paint — one of my favorite smells. I leaned in to the gate and closed my eyes for a moment. That smell always made me happy. Made me forget my worries . . .

Wait! Atlantis was making me forget — again!

I looked down at myself, grabbed the brooch from Shona, and stared at it for a moment — just long enough to remember. Then I shook myself and pushed the gate open. On the other side was a field.

And then the strangest thing happened. I walked through the gate and turned to close it behind me. As I did, I looked back and saw . . .

The cobblestone street had vanished! In its place lay a green field full of white and yellow flowers, all blowing gently in the wind, as if a million daisies were waving me on.

How had that happened?

It didn't matter how it had happened. I had to move on. Closing the gate, I turned back around to the new field — but the field had gone. Now I was looking at a large, busy ice rink! In fact, I wasn't just looking at it. I was standing in the middle of it. On skates.

Crowds of smiling people surrounded me, skating

in circles—holding hands, laughing together, slipping, falling, helping each other up.

I'd never tried ice-skating, but I had always thought it looked like fun. I had once watched a reality TV show where celebrities learned to skate. I'd thought I'd love to give it a try if I ever got the chance. And here I was!

It was almost as if this place knew my secret thoughts and wishes—even the things I'd never said out loud—and somehow brought them to life.

But surely that wasn't possible. It must have been a coincidence.

Either way, I had about two seconds to figure out how to skate before I caused a massive pileup in the middle of the rink.

I stretched out a leg, then the other—and somehow, with barely any effort, I slid smoothly forward. I was doing it! I could skate!

I glided across the ice. I skated forward, backward, spun in circles—it was as if I'd been doing it all my life. It was amazing!

This was *so* much fun—smiling at everyone who passed me, reaching out to take their hands so we could skate together, in time with the music that seemed to be coming from all around us. I wished I could share it with . . .

With . . .

What was his name?

I skated along more nervously now. What was

happening to me? I couldn't remember anyone's names. I had a very vague recollection of friends, parents, teachers, a boyfriend, but they were hazy memories, like shadows, reflections, outlines. Not real.

Your wrist. Look at your wrist.

Something in my brain was urging me to pay attention. I pulled up my sleeve and looked at my wrist. I was wearing a watch. Funny, the time was going backward! 10:41 and 54 seconds. 53, 52, 51.

Why was my watch going backward? Something about it was familiar, but I couldn't remember what it was.

The other wrist.

I rolled my other sleeve up, and the truth slammed into me — just as I slammed into the edge of the rink. Aaron's chain! My boyfriend. Back in . . . back in . . . Where was he? Where was *I*? What was I doing here?

I stumbled off the ice rink. The moment I did, it disappeared behind me as if it had never been there. Suddenly, I was in a square with trees and food stands all around me. People were bustling around, laughing, chatting, nodding, and smiling at one another. Smells wafted from each stand. Oranges, roses, popcorn, cotton candy — every wonderful and delicious smell you could think of. Suddenly, I was desperate for some popcorn.

"There you go, darling." A man handed me a bag without my even asking.

Too stunned to refuse—and it smelled like the freshest, sweetest popcorn I'd ever had in my life—I took it from him and sat down on a bench in front of a fountain.

I'd been warned that Atlantis was magical and dazzling, but I hadn't expected it to be *this* magical—or this bizarre. The popcorn—wow! It was scrumptious!

Wait. Who'd told me about Atlantis? Something was scratching at my mind. Someone had told me about it.

Lyle. That was it.

Of course! I suddenly remembered why I was here. I had a job to do.

As I ate, I pulled out the sheets of paper from my pocket and studied them. To be honest, all I really wanted was to enjoy the moment, but I knew I had to stay strong and remember why I was there. I forced myself to read while I ate my popcorn.

I memorized the faces once again. Then I folded the papers back into my pocket and looked around. There were people everywhere. The ones I wanted to find surely had to be here somewhere, didn't they?

My head was spinning with faces and names and sights and smells—and way too much information. I had to clear my head.

I turned to the fountain, cupped my hands, and filled them with water. I closed my eyes as I splashed the water over my head and face. It was just what I needed—cool and refreshing.

That was better. That was . . .

Wait! Where had the sounds gone?

I opened my eyes. The square had disappeared. I was sitting, alone, on a rock at the edge of a river, my hands still wet from the water.

I staggered to my feet. This place was crazy! How would I ever find anyone here if I couldn't even find my way around?

I rolled up my sleeve. No matter what else happened, I decided I had to keep the chain within sight at all times. I'd make myself look at it constantly, *force* myself to remember. I looked down at my brooch, too, for good measure. Between them, Shona and Aaron had done all they could to keep me safe. The rest was up to me.

I checked my watch: 10:28. Ten and a half hours to go. More than an hour and a half had already passed, and I was getting nowhere, fast.

The cool water had at least cleared my head. I glanced around, pulled myself up from the rock, and set off toward some stepping-stones that led across the river.

As I stepped onto the bridge, I promised myself I wouldn't let myself get sucked in again. Atlantis could try to mess with my head as much as it liked; I wasn't giving up.

I'd find the passengers of *Prosperous II*. I'd bring them all home.

I had a job to do, and I *wasn't* prepared to fail.

Chapter Seventeen

I crossed the bridge and then watched as the river turned into a country lane. I followed the lane, turned a corner, and found myself in the middle of a ballroom, filled with sparkling chandeliers on the ceiling and glowing candlelight coming from every corner. At one end of the room, a huge orchestra was playing. I stood and watched for a moment. A second later, a man in a tuxedo had taken my hand and started waltzing me across the floor!

We spun around and around on the dance floor. I closed my eyes and laughed out loud. When I opened them again, I was in a spinning car on a fairground Tilt-A-Whirl ride. Gasping, I blinked and looked around as the world spun by. Another blink and suddenly I was at the top of a roller coaster. I looked down and saw a city full of the highest skyscrapers. Moments later, I was zooming down into a tunnel that brought me out into a valley full of birdsong and wildflowers.

Every passage took me somewhere even more wonderful and exciting than the last place. Every blink of my eye changed the view. Every door led me into a new land. Every thought I had brought itself to life in front of me.

Among all of this were throngs of smiling, happy people.

But still none that I recognized.

I sat on a cloud that turned into a giant beanbag at the top of a circular slide that had moments earlier been a spiral staircase, and I tried to get my bearings.

I checked the timer on my watch: 08:41. More than three hours gone already. Time was disappearing like sand slipping through my fingers.

I was starting to panic. I could feel it, in my chest, in my thoughts, under my skin. Every bit of me was prickling with question marks and anxiety. I no longer had a plan, no longer had any idea how to get out of this, or the confidence that I could do it at all.

How would I ever find anyone here, when I was almost losing myself? How could I even get from one part of the city to the next when every thought I had turned to . . .

Wait!

My thoughts had been making things happen. The marshmallows, the diamonds sprinkling the water, the waltz becoming a fairground ride. Maybe I could do that with the people, too — think about them and they would appear!

It had to be worth a try.

I clambered out of the beanbag — which turned into an Old English sheepdog, sighed, curled up, and went to sleep — grabbed a burlap bag, sat down on it, and pushed myself down the slide. As I whizzed down and down and around and around, I closed my eyes and went through the list of people in my mind, picturing their faces one by one.

Around the curves I went, wind in my hair, eyes closed, until . . .

"Whoops! Ouch!"

I had landed in the middle of a spongy green field, right at someone's feet.

"I'm so sorry," a voice said as a hand reached down to help me up. "Are you OK?"

"Yes, I'm fine. My fault. Sorry," I garbled as I brushed my legs down and scrambled to my feet. Then I looked up at him. He was vaguely familiar.

Was he one of the *Prosperous II* passengers? Had I found them? Had it worked?

"Are you sure you're all right?" the man asked again. "You seem quite shaken. Here, come and sit down." He pointed to the edge of the field. There was a gate, with a wooden bench on the other side.

We went through the gate.

It led us back into the busy square, or one very similar to it.

The man didn't seem puzzled by the change of scene. He simply sat on a bench in the center of the square and motioned for me to do the same.

"You look as if you've seen a ghost," he said.

"Ha!" I said, trying to keep myself from getting hysterical. "Ha!"

The man looked at me quizzically. As he did, I noticed a scar above his left eye. Yes, he was *definitely* one of the people from the ship—I was sure of it.

He was standing up to go. "Well, if you're sure you're OK . . ." he began.

"No! Wait!" I reached into my pocket and grabbed my sheet of names and faces while the man sat back down.

I ran my finger down the list. He was there! Wavy gray hair, yellow cardigan, green eyes, scar on the left-hand side of his forehead. It was him!

"One second," I urged as I hurriedly scanned the information beside the picture. His name was Tony Mason. He was fifty-seven, and he had a wife named Olivia. She and Tony had just celebrated their silver wedding anniversary. That was why they'd booked the vacation, but Olivia had fallen ill a week before the trip, so he had come with his daughter, Charlotte, instead. There was a photo of Olivia on my sheet.

Tony was looking around, tapping his fingers on his knees, and smiling as a juggler passed by on a unicycle. I glanced up to watch for a moment. The juggler had about fifteen cones all passing in perfect circles through his hands as he cycled. Impossible. Amazing!

It was so easy to get distracted here. I forced myself to concentrate.

"Mr. Mason," I said quietly.

He kept on watching the juggler.

I cleared my throat. "Tony," I said more firmly.

He stopped watching the juggler and turned to me. "How do you know my name?" he asked.

"I . . . um . . ."

"We haven't already met, have we? I'm sure I—"

"No. No, we haven't. You don't know me at all. But I, well, actually, I don't know you, either."

Tony laughed. "Well, that's a good start," he said. "Anyway, I'm always happy to make a new friend. Are you here with your parents?"

I shook my head. "Alone."

Tony frowned. "Well, that's terrible. We must look after you. I'll see if I can find—"

"No, I'm fine." I cut him short.

"Oh. OK." Tony looked shocked. I guessed people didn't interrupt each other in Atlantis.

"Sorry," I went on. "It's just . . . I don't need your help. I've come to help *you*."

Tony stared at me for two seconds, then burst out laughing. "Help me?" he asked. He held his arms out, as if to encompass the square, the fields, the whole island. "How on earth might I be in need of any help? I have everything I could desire."

I swallowed. Could I do it?

Did I have any choice?

"No, you haven't," I said.

"I beg your pardon?"

"You haven't got Olivia," I told him.

"I haven't got who?" he asked, his eyes twinkling as if we were sharing a joke.

I opened up the sheet and held it out to him, pointing at the picture of Olivia. "Your wife."

Tony's eyes twinkled for approximately another nanosecond. Then he took the paper from me. He held it close to his face, then at arm's length. Then he looked at me. Jumping away from the bench as if it were suddenly on fire, he whispered, "Where are you from?" His face had drained of color. "Where *am* I?" he asked, turning in a circle as he scanned the square. "What *is* this place? What's happened to Olivia?"

I didn't know where to start with his questions. Each one could take an hour to answer properly in itself—and we didn't have that kind of time.

"Do you remember her?" I asked instead. "Do you remember your wife?"

"Yes, yes! Of course I remember her. We were going away to celebrate our silver wedding anniversary." Tony flopped back onto the bench. "It was going to be the trip of a lifetime," he went on, "but then Olivia got sick and she told me to go with Charlotte instead." He nodded slowly as he talked, as his real life came back to him.

"There was an accident or something. I don't remember much about it; I was having an afternoon nap. Next thing I knew, I was waking up here."

"So you remember arriving here?" I asked.

He nodded. "As if it were last week."

I decided not to point out that it actually was last week.

"We've been here more than six months now," he went on. "Probably closer to seven. We've made it our home. The only home I thought I had."

Tony turned scared eyes on me. "I abandoned my wife. Charlotte and I forgot all about her! Spent our time laughing and joking and eating fine food, and all the time, poor Olivia . . ." He shook his head, as if to beat away his words. "All that time," he whispered. "She must be beside herself with worry."

"It hasn't been months," I said. He needed to know the truth. "It's been six days."

Tony snorted. "I wish it had been, but you're wrong. We have a whole life here; we have—"

"Time works differently here," I said, interrupting him. "*Everything* works differently here. This is Atlantis."

He stopped, mouth open, and stared at me.

"Look, one thing about time is that we don't have enough of it for me to explain properly," I told him. "But trust me. I'm here to help you get back."

"To Olivia?"

"Yes—if you want to."

"Of course I want to—as long as Charlotte can come, too!"

"I'm hoping that everyone from *Prosperous II* will come, too."

"Good. Just tell me what I need to do."

I reached into my pocket for the other pieces of paper and held them out for him. "Do you know any of these people? They were on the ship with you."

Tony took the bundle of paper from me and flipped through it. "I know all of them," he said. "You've got the crew here, as well as the passengers."

"We need to find them and get them back to the ship."

"What if they don't want to go back?"

"If you just *tell* them about it, they probably *won't*

want to. They'll be like you were. They'll think this is their home and that they're happy here; they won't have any desire to leave. And we can't force them."

"But when they realize they're living in a dream-world, they'll want to go back?" he asked.

"Not just that, but the dream is going to end really soon." I explained about the six days. How at the end of them, they would be gone forever. How their time ended for good at the end of today.

"Then we haven't got a moment to lose." Tony held up the papers. "We show them these?"

"Yes. We need to remind them of their families, tell them their names, show them the photos. All it takes is a glimpse of home and I'm hopeful that they'll remember everything. If you can help me find them, I'm happy to do the talking."

"Of course. Let's do it."

Tony was still flipping through the papers. "Wait, there's one missing," he said. "A young woman, Lowenna. She's not here."

"No. She's different."

Tony tilted his head to the side. "You know, I thought she was. I didn't remember her from the ship — but when I woke up here, she was with us. After the first few days, I didn't question it. I didn't question anything. But why no paperwork for her?"

I put my hand in my pocket and felt for the snow globe Lyle had given me. It was still there. Closing my hand around it, I replied, "I'll look after her—if I can find her."

"We'll find her. We'll find them all. Come on." Tony folded up the paper I'd given him and put it in his pocket.

"Don't do that," I said.

"Don't do what?"

I pointed at his pocket. "Keep it in your hand. You have to keep looking at it."

"Why's that?"

"If you don't, you'll forget again."

Tony laughed. "Forget Olivia again? Never!"

"You'd be surprised. The magic of Atlantis is incredibly strong. Please, don't risk it."

Tony squinted at me for a moment, before nodding in agreement and pulling the paper out of his pocket. "OK," he said, unfolding it and glancing at his wife's photo again. "I won't take anything for granted. Come on. I want to find my daughter."

"Good. And we need to be quick," I said. I checked the countdown on my watch: 08:17. Just over eight hours left! Almost a third of the time was already gone, and I'd found only one passenger. "The ship needs to leave in the next eight hours—or it will *never* get away."

Tony was already hurrying. "I know where most of them hang out. We'll find them."

As we hurried across the square, a question repeated itself over and over in my mind.

Did we really stand a chance of winning this race against time?

But as we dipped through archways in walls that became tunnels through mountains, skipped over rivers on stepping-stones made of giant pearls, edged across bridges that turned into trampolines, and raced along cobblestone streets that twisted and turned like giant writhing snakes, I knew one thing.

The alternative was too terrible to even think about.

Chapter Eighteen

*T*ony was true to his word. He knew where most of the passengers were. An hour later, we'd found nine passengers and most of the crew, including the captain of the ship. There were just three passengers and one crew member still to find. And Lowenna. We hadn't explained anything yet, either. Tony had just told everyone to come with us and that it was important.

We stopped for a break on a piece of headland overlooking a wide pink beach and a sparkling blue bay.

"Dad, are you going to explain what's going on yet?" Tony's daughter, Charlotte, asked.

Tony glanced at me and I nodded. He passed the papers around, and then, between us, we explained everything. I told them about Atlantis, about them being here because they'd been lost at sea, about what would happen at the end of today—and how this was their only chance to get away.

I watched their faces as, one by one, the truth of their "wonderful" lives in Atlantis dawned and they remembered their old lives—their *real* lives. As soon as they'd gotten over the shock of the truth, they wanted to find the other passengers and set sail as soon as possible.

At least, *most* of them did.

A young man who hadn't spoken yet put up his hand.

"What is it, Alan?" Tony asked.

Alan waved his piece of paper at us and shrugged. "What if I don't want to leave?" he asked.

"Don't want to leave?" Tony repeated incredulously. "Have you been listening for the last half an hour? Do you know where you are? Do you remember your old life, your *real* life?"

Alan shrugged again. "Yes, on all counts," he said flatly. He held up the photo on his piece of paper. "And yes, I *completely* remember the day my fiancée walked out on me. It was the same month that I lost my job, and a couple of days after our home was foreclosed."

No one spoke for a moment. The air stilled and tightened.

Eventually, as softly as a summer breeze, Alan added, "Why would I want to go back to that?"

One of the women went over to Alan and stroked his arm. "That's awful," she said. "You poor thing."

"Thanks, Jenna," Alan mumbled.

Tony frowned. "Alan, Atlantis isn't what you think. It's . . ."

Alan shook his head. "I'm sorry, guys. You go if you like. I'm staying here."

I looked at Tony. Could we let Alan stay when we had the chance to help him get away? A chance that according to Lyle had virtually never happened before. A chance to choose life.

Tony spoke softly. "You're not staying," he said.

"I like it here!" Alan insisted. "I've never been so happy anywhere, never had so many friends, never—"

"Where are your friends now, Alan?" Tony asked. "Not us, or the people who came here after us. Where are the ones who came *before* us?"

Alan stared at him. "They . . ." His face clouded with confusion. "That's a thought," he murmured. "Where have they gone?"

"My dad's right," Charlotte said. "The group from

the *Eclipse*—remember? The ship that got here a week before us. Anyone seen any of them lately?"

One of the older men spoke up. "None of those guys have been around for days, now that I think about it," he said.

"What about the crew of that sailboat—what was it called?" Tony went on.

"The *Blue Typhoon*?" Charlotte offered.

"That's it," Tony replied. "Where are they? Gone. Those two canoeists? The guys from the racing yacht? The people from that fancy cruise ship? All of them gone. *No one* who arrived before us is here anymore."

"But where are they, then?" Alan asked. "What happened to them?"

Jenna cleared her throat. "I think we all know in our hearts what happened to them. Think of the night the *Eclipse* guys went. They were here that evening—probably at their most cheerful, all of them. Then later that night, the sky had a whole lot more stars in it. Remember? We commented on it?"

A few in the group nodded, remembering something that Atlantis had since made them forget.

"I can't be positive—but I think those stars were them," Jenna went on. "All I know for sure is that the next morning, they were gone. Maybe there was some dust on the ground, maybe an extra flower bloomed that day for each of them. I don't know. All I *do* know is that we never saw them again. The end of the road came for each of them—like it will come for us, too."

"Jenna's right. The same thing happened when the canoeists went," Charlotte said. "I'd completely forgotten, but I remember it now. Two bright stars came out that night—lit up the whole island for an hour or two."

"And at the end of today, you'll be the same," I said. "You won't get to stay here anymore—any of you. You won't have the choice to try to go home. This is your only chance."

"You've heard her. In a few hours, it's game over," Tony said flatly. "That's the truth of it. This here"—he waved his arms across the headland, across the bay, the island, all of it—"it's a holding place. We're nowhere. We're between worlds. It's an illusion. Come tonight, there's no more *between* and no more Atlantis. You'll be gone, and that's the end of it. Alan, if you need me to spell it out for you, I will. At the end of today, time's up. You'll be *dead*."

Alan's face had drained of color.

"So. Your choice." Tony stared at him. "Are you coming with us, or are we leaving you here to die alone?"

Alan didn't speak for a moment. *No one* spoke. The air seemed to be stretched so tight, it felt as if it would splinter into pieces.

Eventually, Alan muttered, "I guess a crummy life is better than no life at all."

I let out a breath. Thank goodness. I looked at my timer: 07:03. Almost five hours had passed; we had just seven hours left.

Tony went over and shook Alan's hand. "Good man. We'll look after you," he promised.

"All right. Come on," I said. "We need to find the others and get back to the ship.

"I bet I know where Alex and Phil are," one of the women said. "There's a garden they always go in the afternoons. And Gabi is Alex's best friend. She might be with them. If not, they'll probably know where to find her. I'll go get them."

"Great." Tony said. He rifled through his papers and handed her three sheets. "Make sure you give them these."

"And keep looking at the pictures of your own family on your way," I added. "It's easy to forget here." Which, as I said it, reminded me. "What about Lowenna?" I asked.

The captain came over to me. "I'll show you how to find her," he said. "She's with Miriam, my final crew member. There's a park you can find when you know how. They'll be there."

Tony took charge. "OK, great. The captain can go with Emily. Jeanette is fetching the others. Everyone else, come with me. Get your stuff and we'll head back to the ship together. Let's all meet there, say, on the top deck in an hour?"

"Wait!" I yelled. Tony had reminded me of the

final essential detail. Everyone turned to look at me.

"There's one last thing," I said. "You can't take anything with you. Anything you got in Atlantis — clothes, food, jewelry, whatever it is — you must leave it behind."

"Why's that?" a young woman asked.

"If you attempt to leave Atlantis with something *of* Atlantis, the ship won't be able to get away," I explained.

As I said the words, I remembered that they applied to me, too. I pulled the garland from around my head, realizing as I did so that it hadn't been just a gift to make me smile, it had been a way of helping to root me in Atlantis — to ease the transition, take away any memories that would remind me of what I'd lost, and keep me here. "Things like this," I said. "Anything that comes from here, you have to leave it behind."

"Darn it. That blows my idea of taking presents back for the grandkids," one of the older men mumbled.

"Their present will be seeing their grandparents return alive, Louie," his wife replied, nudging him and pointing at the beautiful gold watch on his arm. "That was from here, too. Off it goes."

"Just leave it all here," Tony said. "Someone else will have a nice treat when they go for a walk on the headland."

I unclasped my diamond bracelet and put it on the ground. As I did, I sent a wish with it—that it would bring someone a feeling of warmth and happiness in their final days here. That it would bring a smile to the face of someone whose time really was up.

I checked my timer: 06:47. We still had nearly seven hours. "OK," I said. "Let's go."

The captain and I left the square together. He told me to call him Phil. "I know a shortcut," he said as he strode ahead. I had to run to keep up with him.

We left the square behind us, and I followed him up a tiny, winding street. Like all the other roads, it was cobblestone and quaint. On each side, gleaming white houses had wooden shutters and walls painted in pastel colors. They were so pretty that under any other circumstances, I would have wanted to take my time, strolling along and admiring each one.

Phil broke into my thoughts. "OK, are you ready for the shortcut?" he asked.

"I guess so," I replied, wondering why I had to be ready. I was just following him, wasn't I?

"See that wall at the top of the road?" he asked.

I looked ahead and saw that the road was blocked

by a huge brick wall with a colorful mural painted on it.

"Oh." I stopped walking. "Why are we going up here? It's a dead end."

"Look at the wall," Phil urged me. "What do you see?"

I stared at the mural. "Um. A picture of a house with a ladder leaning against it. A man at the top of the ladder cleaning a window." I studied it further. "Very lifelike, isn't it?"

"Exactly. That was what I thought when I first saw it. It's *so* lifelike that in fact . . ." Phil pointed at the wall. "You see the door right down at the bottom, near the base of the ladder?"

I looked where he was pointing. There was a bright-red door with a gleaming brass handle. It was so bright, it could have just been painted that day. "I see it."

"You have to grab that handle—it'll take you through."

"But it's not a real handle; it's a painting," I protested.

Phil just looked at me. "And this is Atlantis," he said by way of explanation.

He was right. Much weirder things than walking through a picture of a door in a wall had happened since I'd arrived here. We continued walking.

"You have to be confident. Walk up to the wall,

reach out for the door handle, and it will come to life in your hand. As soon as you feel it tingle, turn it and the door will open. Ready?"

"I guess."

The captain stopped. "Hold on! I tried it with someone else the other day and it didn't work. I went through but my friend didn't."

"You think it might not work for me, either?"

He shook his head. "It's not that. I've tested it a few times. It will let only one person through. You go. I'll wait here for a few minutes, make sure you've really gone. If you don't come back, I'll assume it's worked and I'll see you back on the ship. Are you ready?"

My heart quickened. Not just from the fear of literally walking into a wall, but because of what was on the other side. Was I actually going to meet Lowenna?

"Yeah, I'm ready," I said. And then I strode toward a brick wall, reached out for a picture of a brass handle, and walked straight through a door that a moment ago had been a few splashes of paint.

I opened my eyes and gazed around me. I was surrounded by the most stunning beauty. To one side of me, a field of flowers spread in swirling patterns as far as I could see: bright red, deep blue, dazzling yellow, pure white—they were everywhere. The air was full of their scent, too. It smelled as though someone had invented the ultimate, perfect perfume.

On the other side of me, a bridge emerged from the wildflowers to cross a river that danced and sparkled like the finest jewels.

Behind me, what had been a wall was now a line of trees, the sun glinting between their branches as though they were full of dancing fairies.

Ahead, the river opened up into a pool. Above it, the highest waterfall I'd ever seen snaked through rocks and trees, to fall into the water below in a shimmering curtain. Next to the pool, someone was lying on a rock in the sunshine.

Lowenna.

I approached the pool, stepping carefully across the rocks till I reached the one she was lying on.

"Lowenna?" I whispered, reaching out to touch her shoulder.

She stirred at my touch. "What? What's wrong?" She sat up, squinting into the sunlight. Then her eyes focused on me. "Who are you?"

"I . . . I'm Emily," I said simply.

"Wait." She reached out toward me, traced my face with her hand. "I know you," she whispered. "Don't I?"

I wasn't sure how to answer. Our previous meeting—touching palms across a porthole window—hadn't exactly been your average way of getting to know someone.

I got as far as "I . . . um . . ." when she sat up and stared at me, squinting. "You're familiar, but I can't think where from. You're not from Atlantis, are you?"

I realized how to answer her questions. I didn't need words. I had something that would do a better job than any explanation I could give her.

I reached into my pocket and pulled out the snow globe from Lyle. As I held it out toward her, Lowenna gasped and covered her mouth with her hands.

Then she gently took the globe from me. "No! I don't believe it. Surely it can't be. . . ."

She lowered her head, gripping the snow globe tightly, as if it were a long-lost family heirloom. As I watched her, I saw a tear drip onto it from her face.

I awkwardly reached out to her. "Are you OK?" I asked, touching her arm.

Lowenna nodded and looked up at me. She wiped her wet cheek with the back of a hand. "It's just a shock to realize that it happened to me," she said. "We always thought we were immune."

"From Atlantis?"

Lowenna nodded. "How long has it been?" she asked urgently. "In your world—how long?"

"Um. The day you disappeared was last Friday."

"So last Friday was day one?"

I nodded. "This is day six."

Lowenna turned as white as the froth from the waterfall behind her. "Day six?"

I nodded. "Lyle said after today . . ."

"I know!" Lowenna held a hand up to stop me. Her face had softened with emotion. "My Lyle," she said huskily. "How is he?"

I thought about the state he'd been in all week. The sunken eyes, unwashed clothes, pale skin. But then I thought about the glimmer of hope he'd had this morning when he came to see me off. Was it really only this morning? It felt like days ago. "He's fine," I said. "He wants you home."

"I tried so hard," she said. "The ship was in bad shape when we arrived. To be honest, it took me at least the first day to recover from the shock that I had come through with it."

"Do you know why you did?" I asked.

Lowenna took a breath and closed her eyes. "I just know I got caught up in the earthquake. I was too close to the ship when it hit. I didn't stand a chance. None of us did." Her voice cracked as she spoke.

"I'm sorry. You don't have to talk about it," I said.

"No. It's good to talk about it. I need to remember." She put her hand on my arm. "Have we got much time?"

I checked the countdown: 06:23. We had nearly six and a half hours. "A little."

Lowenna motioned to a set of stepping-stones that led across the river to the other side. "Come on. Let's talk as we walk. We need to go this way."

"What about Miriam?" I asked. "The captain said she'd be with you."

"That's where we're going now," Lowenna replied as she reached out to help me across the rocks. "We'll pick her up on the way." Then she pointed at my wrist—at my chain from Aaron.

"Is that your snow globe?" she asked.

"Yes."

"Good. It's important."

"I know. So go on," I said as I hopped from the rocks to the other side of the river. "What happened next? After you got here?"

"The ship was badly broken," she went on as we walked. "Because of my work, I knew that we had a matter of days to fix things before we would stop wanting to . . . before Atlantis drew us in. Most of the others left even before that—completely bewitched by the magic of Atlantis. Some stayed behind with me, but then they gradually drifted away."

"So you tried to fix the ship?"

"*Tried* is the word, yes. The engines were damaged, but I managed to get a few volunteers to help mend the sails. Once we'd done that, we made our first attempt to get back—but we failed."

Their first attempt. That would have been one of the times we'd seen them from Fivebays Island.

"My companions weren't strong enough to keep trying, though," Lowenna went on. "Certainly not strong enough to counter the magic that Atlantis was weaving around us. I was soon fighting a losing battle—except with the captain."

"Phil? Why was he different?"

"That's what I kept asking myself. My best guess was that he was a seagoing man who'd worked on ships all his life. Perhaps he'd built up some kind of immunity. I don't know. I just know that he held out longer against Atlantis."

"But not long enough?"

"No. We worked together for . . . I don't know how long. We made a couple more attempts to escape. The sails were too weak to get us far, but we'd started to fix the engines. They were working intermittently. Meanwhile, I spent every waking hour working on my calculations for our course home. We were so close."

"So what happened?"

"Phil succumbed like the others. He fought it—told me to remind him of his wife and kids, which I did regularly. But in the end, my words weren't enough."

"No. You need something you can see or touch, like a photo." I held up my wrist. "Or like this."

Lowenna studied me. "You've done a lot of home-work, haven't you?"

I shrugged. "Lyle did most of it."

She nodded. "Anyway, that's about it. Once the captain was gone and I was the only one left to try to get us home, the job was almost impossible. Soon after that, I lost my way. I was the only one still on the ship. I grew desperate. Scared."

"That's probably when I saw you," I said.

Lowenna stopped. "Yes," she whispered. "I remember everything now. You were at the window! You were outside the porthole."

I nodded. "That was how I knew you hadn't gone for good."

"I wasn't far off. It wasn't much later that I succumbed to Atlantis, too." She held her arms out wide. "You've got to admit—it's hard to resist." Lowenna reached out and squeezed my hand. Then, almost echoing Lyle's words, she said, "You know I will never be able to thank you enough for this, don't you?"

"I haven't done anything yet," I said. "The hardest part is still ahead of us."

"You're right. We need to get going. We haven't got long."

I checked the timer: 05:52. Less than six hours left! Time was running out so fast. "No. We haven't got long at all!"

Lowenna quickened her pace. "Have you got all of the others?"

I nodded. "The others should all be there by the time we get back to the ship."

"Just us and Miriam to go, then," Lowenna replied as she led the way into a copse of trees. "Come on, she'll be around here."

I followed Lowenna into the trees. Leaves crinkled

beneath us as we walked. The birdsong under the trees was like an orchestra of pipe music. It was heavenly.

Ahead of us, a woman was pacing back and forth. She had something held against her shoulder.

"Miriam!" Lowenna called out. The woman turned. As she did, I could see what she was holding. A baby!

"Miriam has a baby?" I asked.

Lowenna laughed, her eyes lighting up and dancing in a way I hadn't seen until now. "The baby isn't Miriam's," she said as she reached out her arms and Miriam passed the bundle to her. "Miriam was helping out so I could have a nap. The baby is mine."

I stared at the tiny little face with eyes that were shut tight, a scrunchy little nose, and a frowning, twitching mouth.

"Mine and Lyle's," Lowenna added. "This is our baby girl."

"I — I didn't know you had a baby," I said, staring into its little face. "Lyle didn't tell me."

Lowenna paused. "Lyle didn't know," she said quietly.

"But how . . . ?"

"I was going to tell him that night. I had a whole celebration planned," Lowenna said dreamily.

"That night? Last week?"

"Last week for you, yes. For me it was nearly seven months ago. She's ten days old."

I let out a breath. It was one thing being *told* that time worked differently in Atlantis. But to see proof like this—well, that just blew me away.

It did another thing, too: it made me even more determined to make this work. Lyle had a daughter and he didn't even know it! We had to get Lowenna and her baby back home where they belonged. We *had* to.

I leaned over to take a closer look at the baby. As I did, she opened her eyes and gurgled at me. "What's her name?"

Lowenna grimaced. "She doesn't have a name yet. I know, I know. It's terrible. I just—even though I was losing sight of my real life, I think a part of me was holding on to it strongly enough to believe that I would get back there one day—and I didn't want to name her until she'd met her daddy. It felt wrong, somehow. I call her 'my treasure.'"

I reached out a finger to stroke the baby's face. "I understand," I said. "And she's going to meet her daddy. I'll make sure of it."

Lowenna smiled at me. "Come on," she said softly. "Let's go join the others. We can explain everything to Miriam on the way back to the ship."

As the three of us walked, as I passed Miriam a sheet of paper with a picture of her own sons on it, and as Lowenna and I explained our plans, my determination grew stronger and stronger.

We had just over five hours to do it, but nothing would stop us now. We were getting away from Atlantis — tonight.

Chapter Nineteen

*I*t wasn't working.

Lowenna, Miriam, the baby, and I had gotten back to the ship as fast as we could and met up with the others on the top deck. After a final roll call to check that everyone was on board, we'd gotten down to work.

The captain had a few more nuts and bolts to adjust — things he hadn't fixed before he'd lost himself to Atlantis. He spent about an hour down on the lower deck with a couple of the other men, and between them, they got the engines going again.

Meanwhile, Lowenna put all her navigational charts in order and plotted the complicated route home.

The passengers had pulled up all the ropes, closed all the doors, fastened down everything loose, tidied up the spillages and mayhem all around the ship. The engines were in working order. This was it. We were ready to leave.

But we weren't going anywhere. The ship wouldn't budge.

We even tried hoisting the sails. Nothing.

We all gathered on the top deck. All except the captain. He was still inside, trying to get us going.

"What's the matter? Why aren't we moving?" one of the women asked. She was an older lady with white hair, on the ship with her husband, who was sitting next to her. "Have we checked the anchor?" she asked. "It's not stuck, is it?"

"We've checked the anchor, Ruth," Lowenna replied. "It's not that, and it's not the sails or the engine, either. I've charted our route. We all know it's going to be a complicated journey — and not one that many would manage to follow — but we've put all the coordinates into the computers, and our captain is one of the best there is. We should be on our way. I don't know what's stopping us."

I checked my countdown watch: 03:37. Less than a third of the time I'd started with. How had that happened so quickly? I could feel a flickering in my body, as though a panicked fish were flapping around inside my stomach.

"Are you all absolutely positive you haven't brought anything back to the ship from Atlantis?" I asked. "Gifts for your family? Little trinkets? Chocolates? *Anything?*"

"We've checked all the cabins and all the communal spaces and there's nothing anywhere," one of the men, Charlie, said. "Anything we found was either left behind on the island or has been thrown from the ship."

"We've even frisked one another to make sure there's nothing in our clothes!" added Tony.

"It doesn't make sense. We should be moving," Lowenna mused. She jiggled the baby as she talked, staring out to sea and murmuring as she thought aloud. "The ship's fixed, the route is mapped, we have nothing here from Atlantis . . ."

And then, as I watched her bounce her beautiful baby on her hip, it hit me. The moment it did, I wished with all my might that I was wrong—but I knew I wasn't.

"You have." My voice came out as a croak.

"Huh?" Lowenna turned to me. The baby gurgled as she moved.

I cleared my throat. "You have something from Atlantis," I said, forcing unwelcome words out through an unwilling throat.

I kept my eyes focused on Lowenna. As she gazed back at me, I saw the truth dawn in her eyes.

Lowenna's face drained of color. "No," she whispered. "No!" Wrapping both arms so tightly around her baby, I was almost afraid she'd squash her, she stood there, shaking her head, and repeating the word, over and over again. "No. No. No. No."

Miriam came over to Lowenna and put a hand on her arm. "What is it?" she asked. "What's wrong?"

Lowenna continued shaking her head. Tears fell from her face onto the bundle in her arms.

"It's the baby," I said hoarsely.

"I don't understand," Miriam insisted. "What about the baby?"

"She was born here!" Lowenna cried. Her voice was like the howl of an injured animal. "She's from Atlantis. As long as she is on the ship, we can *never* escape!"

I wasn't sure how long we stood in silence after that. Actually, I had a fairly reasonable guess. My countdown watch was saying 03:16. Just over three hours to go, and we had discovered a problem I had no idea how to solve. I wasn't sure that there *could* be a solution.

"I'm not leaving her behind," Lowenna said, clutching her baby tightly to her chest. "I'm not leaving her."

One of the other younger women came forward and put an arm around Lowenna's shoulders. "No one is suggesting you leave her behind," she reassured her. "No one would even think it."

"Sally, I know. But then we can *never* get away," Lowenna said. "Unless . . ." She paused. "Unless you go without me. We'll stay here. I've given the captain everything he needs to get back. You can do it."

"You're not staying behind," I said. "You know that after today, there will never be a way back." I thought of Lyle's pale, gray face, his dark eyes, the hope I'd seen in them when he waved me off. "You're not staying behind," I repeated more firmly.

"But there's no other way," Lowenna insisted. "Better for you to leave us behind than for *everyone* to be stuck here forever."

"There must be another way," I insisted. "There *has* to be." My brain was working double time. There was something here. A solution. I could sense it, almost feel it, itching the corners of my mind. Numbers, hours, baby, portal . . .

I could feel Lowenna beside me as I thought, her baby in her arms, rocking her, soothing her, whispering comforting thoughts, when really she was the one who needed comforting.

"You know, it's strange," she said as she looked

at her baby. "She's always had this little worried look on her face. Always a little frown. I thought it was just the shape of her face—but maybe it was this. Maybe, somehow, she knew. My baby knew all along. Knew we were doomed." Lowenna's voice broke, and a tear slipped down her cheek and onto the baby's head.

"Hey, shush, now. Don't say things like that," Miriam murmured. "No one's doomed. We'll sort this out. We'll think of a solution."

Lowenna shook her head. "There is no solution," she cried. "I can't bear it. My love for my husband and my love for my baby, pulling me in opposite directions—and me torn into two pieces between them.

Wait! That was it!

"No one needs to stay behind!" I said. "We can *all* get back home. I've got an idea."

Everyone hushed and came closer as I explained my plan. "There's a portal. That's how I got here. It will open again in"—I checked my watch: 02:51—"less than three hours. It will stay open for as long as the slack tide and the dusk are in tune."

"How long is that?" a man asked.

"I don't know. A matter of minutes. You lose track of time when you're going through the portal."

"Makes about as much sense as everything else around here," one of the men mumbled.

"Exactly," I agreed. "All I know is that I was

thrown around in a swirling tunnel of lights and electricity and . . ." I glanced at Lowenna. She was holding the baby even closer. I decided she didn't need *too* much description of the journey. "Anyway, there isn't long—but there's long enough."

"Long enough for what?" Ruth asked.

"To get back," I said.

"You mean you're not going to come with us on the ship?" she asked.

I shook my head. "It's not for me. Or at least, it *was.*" I looked at Lowenna again. I could see she knew where I was going.

"You'd let *us* use the portal?" she breathed.

"It's a loophole. A glitch in Atlantis's armor. A back door to sneak through without anyone knowing. It's all about 'between' states. The dusk and the slack tide are two. You have to have two more between states for it to work." I turned to Lowenna. "You're a semi-mer, like me."

"That's one," Lowenna said. "What's the other?"

"You just said it, yourself. Your situation is making you have to choose between going home to your husband or staying here with your baby. You can't possibly pick one over the other—you're stuck *between* the two."

"You think that will work?" the captain asked. "It's enough to get her through this portal?"

"It's the best chance I can think of," I said. "But it's up to Lowenna."

"I'll try it," she said instantly. "I'll try anything. But what about the rest of you?"

"What about us?" Ruth asked.

"What if I abandon you and the ship can't make it back? You'll hit a massive magnetic resistance as you leave, and then again when you're nearing the point where the earthquake took us through. It could be devastating—and I won't be there to help guide you through it. What if I return home and the rest of you are stuck here forever? I couldn't live with that."

"Everything is in place. You've said so yourself. The ship *will* make it back"—I glanced down at the baby, now sleeping in her mother's arms, blissfully unaware of the drama being played out around her—"as long as this little piece of Atlantis isn't on board."

Lowenna nodded.

"What if *they* don't make it back?" Sally asked. "What if you're wrong about this 'between' thing?"

"I'm willing to take that risk," Lowenna answered. "It's got to be worth a try—as long as I have my baby with me."

"This is the best chance of *all* of us getting home," I said, catching Alan's eye. "I don't know about the rest of you, but I'm not prepared to leave *anyone* behind."

Alan nodded at me. "We all agree," he said. "It's the best option."

Lowenna came over to my side and put an arm around me. "It's a risk for all of us, but you're right, it's our best chance—possibly our *only* chance." She looked around at the group. "Come on," she said. "Let's get ready to try again."

Lowenna said emotional good-byes to the others, then she and I went down to her cabin together. As we reached her corridor, we edged into the water. Lowenna's legs did the same as mine: they melted away, fused together, and turned into a beautiful, silvery tail.

Lowenna held out her baby, half in the water and half above it. A few minutes later, the same thing happened. Her teeny little legs were replaced by a tiny pink tail.

I think she was the cutest thing I'd ever seen.

Lowenna saw me looking and smiled. "Clever little thing, isn't she?"

"She's swishy!"

"OK, let's go," Lowenna said, and we swam to her cabin.

The ship's timer had been synchronized with my watch, so we were counting down together: 00:12. Twelve minutes to go. Nearly there.

If everything worked as it should, in twelve

minutes the window in Lowenna's cabin would turn into a portal, and she and her baby girl would swim through it and back to the real world.

The moment they were gone, the ship should start to move. *Should.* What if it didn't? What if I was stuck here forever? What if I never saw Shona again, or Aaron or Mandy or Mom and Dad or—?

"Emily." Lowenna broke into my thoughts.

"Huh? Yeah, what?"

"You're sure about this?"

"Of course," I replied without hesitating. I didn't want to share my fears with her, not at this stage. "Are you?"

Lowenna nodded. "Look. If it doesn't . . . If I don't get back . . ."

"You *will* get back. Don't talk like that."

"I know. I'm sure everything will be fine, but just in case . . . *If* I don't get back, if it doesn't work, will you do something for me?"

"Of course I will. Anything."

"Tell Lyle about our daughter. Tell him she had his eyes. Tell him she already loved him as much as I did. Tell him I'm—"

"It won't be necessary," I interrupted. I couldn't bear to hear her talk like this, as though she and the baby had already failed, as though they were already things of the past.

"Just tell him I'm sorry," she insisted. "I'm sorry I didn't get to tell him about her myself. And I'm sorry I messed up. Tell him to be happy. Will you do that for me?"

I nodded. I couldn't speak.

Lowenna reached out and stroked my cheek. "You're a brave girl," she said softly. Something about the way she spoke reminded me of my mom, and I was instantly hit with a lurch of homesickness that felt like a fist in my stomach.

"How much time is left?" she asked.

I showed her the timer on my watch: 00:04.

"Four minutes," she said. "Are you ready?"

How could I be ready for this? I mean, I'd faced Neptune in a bad mood, a sea monster waking up on the wrong side of the bed, an evil tyrant frozen into a mountain—but somehow none of them had scared me as much as this. It wasn't only *my* life at stake here; it was a shipful of people's lives—including one that had only just begun. "Yeah," I lied. "I'm ready."

I gave the baby a kiss on her head and wrapped my arms around Lowenna. "Good luck," I breathed into her shoulder.

"You too." She hugged me hard, then pulled away to hold me at arm's length. "I'll see you on the other side."

I hope so, I thought. *I really hope so.*

00:02. Two minutes to go.

"Look." I pointed at the porthole. It had started shimmering as it had when I came onto the ship—

lighting up with a hundred colors, vibrating, buzz-ing. Was that only twelve hours ago? It already felt like more like a week.

The porthole hummed. I could feel the electricity from here.

00:01. One minute left.

Lowenna smiled at me, then clutching her baby mergirl in her arms, she turned away, ducked below the water, and swam toward the waiting portal.

Chapter Twenty

*T*ime was up. 00:00.

I watched from inside the cabin. The porthole disappeared, and in its place was a myriad of colors. It looked as if the glass had splintered into a million pieces and each piece was held up to the sun. Bright colors burned through it so hard I had to close my eyes against the glare.

The cabin shook. It felt as if I were in a rocket about to launch, or in the center of an earthquake. I curled into a ball and felt myself spinning through the water as wave after wave of energy exploded and crackled and burned all around me.

Lowenna and the baby — they were right in the heart of the explosions. How could they survive?

I opened my eyes and squinted into the light. I could still see them: the tips of their tails disappearing into the maelstrom, spinning in circles, caught up in the blazing explosion of the portal.

I forced my eyes to stay open, despite the burning of the lights. I could still see something moving inside the lights. Was that a tail? Were they OK? When would it end?

Come on, come on, get through!

I stared at the retreating dot of Lowenna's tail for another minute. And then — it stopped.

Just like that.

A loud *whoosh!* A final burst of light. A fizzing of energy — and the portal closed like an elevator's door.

I was alone.

Reeling and shaking, I swam across to the porthole. It was completely intact. There was no sign that anything strange had been going on at all. Outside, there was only the darkness of the ocean.

And that wasn't all. I listened hard and I could just hear it — the *dunka, dunka, dunka* of the ship's engines.

We were moving.

We were leaving Atlantis.

I just hoped and prayed with every bit of me that Lowenna and her baby girl were, too.

The trouble started almost immediately.

I had left Lowenna's cabin and was in the corridor when the ship lurched violently to one side. Water rushed over me, and I soon found myself swimming through what felt like a thundering, rolling wave.

Somehow, I made it to the end of the corridor. I gripped the handrail at the bottom of the staircase, holding on with both hands as my body was hurled from side to side. Water sloshed around me. I climbed a couple of steps up, out of the water, and my tail thrashed violently as it stung and tingled and finally turned back into my legs.

Through the windows at the side of the ship, I could see the sky one minute, the sea the next. It felt as if there were giants on either side of us, rocking the boat violently, like a pair of school bullies slamming a seesaw up and down while the kids in the middle clung on for dear life.

Not just that, but the light was constantly shifting. One moment, it was like bright sunlight; the next, the sky filled with black clouds and the sea turned dark. It was as if night and day, sunshine and storms, hope and betrayal, were all mixed in together.

I could see someone farther up the staircase, hanging on to the handrail. It was the white-haired lady, Ruth.

"Emily!" she screamed. "Are you OK?"

"I'm fine!" I yelled back. "What's happening?"

"I think it's the resistance that Lowenna mentioned. I'm sure we'll be through it soon. Just stay calm and hold on tight!"

I tried to do what she said. I held on as tightly as I could, closing my eyes and praying it would soon end. As I prayed, the ship continued to rock and reel and throw us this way and that, like an angry child with a toy it no longer wanted.

"Emily."

Someone was shaking me. I clutched the rail even more tightly. *No! No, don't . . .*

"Emily, look."

I opened my eyes. Ruth was smiling at me. She pointed to the window.

I moved my head to see where she was pointing. Sea. Water. Just the ocean. No mountainous waves, no storms. I looked back at Ruth. "We made it," I whispered. "We got away."

She reached out to help me up. "Thanks to you, we did," she said. "We're heading home."

I clung to Ruth's arm as we climbed up to the top deck together.

I could see a group of people huddled together inside the cabin in the middle of the deck. We made our way over to them.

Sally came running out. "Emily! Ruth!" She pulled us into the huddle. "Are you OK?" she asked softly.

"She's fine," Ruth answered for me.

"Are Lowenna and the baby all right?" another woman asked.

"Hey, hey." Tony waved his arms in a *slow down* kind of way. "Give the child a chance to answer."

I looked around at them all, every eye on me. "I'm OK," I said. "But I — I don't know about Lowenna and the baby. They disappeared into the portal. They got off the ship. That's why we're moving."

As if in reply, the ship took a sudden lurch to the left and I fell against Ruth. We'd escaped the storms, but there were still heavy seas out there.

I straightened myself up. "I can't say for sure what happened after that," I went on. "I have no idea if they'll get home or not. That portal is vicious."

I shuddered as I recalled my own experience

of going through it—and thought of Lowenna's retreating body disappearing into the unknown. "It's like a black hole that could swallow you up without a trace," I muttered.

I looked around at the others, suddenly—and yes, perhaps a bit belatedly—realizing that maybe they wanted to hear good news, not my inner fears!

"But, look, I'm sure they'll be OK," I added quickly.

Ruth smiled at me. "There's nothing we can do now. We're on our way home, and whatever else happens, we will *always* be grateful to them—and to you—for that."

"Hear, hear!" her husband said.

The others nodded. A couple of them even clapped. Sally smiled at me. "Well done, Emily. You're a brave, brave girl."

I tried to smile back. But as the ship creaked and thumped and banged, and as we continued to veer from side to side and lurch up and down, and as our journey still felt long and hard and dangerous, I couldn't help wondering where on earth she'd gotten the idea that I was anything other than a scared child who wanted to go home.

Things were starting to change. The sea was growing rougher.

Lowenna had warned us this would happen. It was the second wave of resistance. It meant we were nearing the end of our journey; we were approaching the point where the earthquake had swallowed the ship.

Lowenna had given the captain everything he needed to get through, every coordinate, every instruction. But without a Way Maker to guide us home, we needed one more ingredient: luck.

The snippets of brightness were giving way to black clouds. The sea was developing enormous waves, peaking like mountains, white water streaming across their tops like snow.

Up the mountains we climbed, gripping on to one another for dear life. Then we teetered on the cusp of the wave—like that moment at the top of a roller coaster when you're about to leave your stomach behind—and down we crashed.

Over and over. Clambering dangerously up, crashing fiercely down. Water spilled over the deck from every side; chairs that hadn't been bolted down slid violently across the wet deck, over the side, and out to sea.

The sky clapped and roared; a raging thunderstorm followed our every move, folded us inside itself as it lifted us up, hurled us down, screaming its violent anger at us.

I had never been so close to a thunderstorm before, and I had never seen one as wild as this— not even on Neptune's angriest days.

On and on it went, unrelenting in its rage.

One thought kept repeating over and over in my mind: after everything we'd been through, were we going to be hurled from our boat out here—fail at the last hurdle?

It was the last thought in my mind as another wave struck us and I fell to the deck.

Was it the last thought I would ever have?

I must have blacked out. I think we all did, because next thing I knew, we were all opening our eyes, looking around at one another, and picking ourselves up.

Was it over? Had we come through it? *Were we alive?*

My legs felt wobbly as I stood up. Every limb felt bruised. Every muscle ached.

But I didn't care about that.

"Look!" One of the men was pointing out to sea. A few of the others had already run to the side of the ship.

As I went over to join them, I realized two things. Thing one: The ship was completely level. We were sailing on the calmest seas I had ever seen. You'd hardly even know we were moving.

Thing two: Up ahead and a little to the right, I could see land. And not just any land.

Fivebays Island.

Chapter Twenty-One

*M*y good-byes were swift. After a round of tearful hugs and "good luck's" and "we'll never forget you's," I dived from the ship. One last wave to the others and I ducked under the water and swam as fast as I could back to the island.

A couple of long, sleek silver fish swam on either side of me, as if they had been sent to escort me home. We raced along the channel together, zooming through the clear, smooth water. I couldn't help smiling all the way. We'd done it! We'd really done it.

All I could think about was seeing Lyle reunited with his wife and meeting his daughter for the first time.

The light was fading as I approached Fivebays Island. I swam above the water and looked across at Sandy Bay. I could just about make out three figures on the beach. I stopped swimming and waved. One of them waved back, then nudged the others. A moment later, two of the figures had run down to the water's edge and dived right in. The other waited on the sand. As I got closer, I could see that it was Mandy.

It didn't take long to find out who the others were.

"Emily!" Aaron was swimming toward me at the speed of a rocket. "Emily! You're back! You're back!" He swam at me so hard, I almost did a backward somersault under the water. Once I'd recovered, he grabbed me and held me tightly. I hugged him back just as hard. It felt as if we'd been apart for months.

Lyle was right behind him. I grinned at him. I couldn't wait to hear how he'd felt when he'd seen Lowenna, and what he thought about his daughter!

And then he said something that took all the happy out of everything.

"Is Lowenna with you?"

I let go of Aaron. "What?"

"Lowenna? Where is she?"

"Isn't she back?" I asked stupidly. Of course she

wasn't back. If she were back, he wouldn't be asking if she was with *me*. Where was she, then?

I watched the hope drain out of Lyle's face, leaving it gray and lifeless. Worse, even, than it had been before I'd gone.

"What do you mean?" he asked. "She isn't with you?"

"She . . . she came separately," I said carefully. I couldn't tell him about the baby. That was for Lowenna to do. When she got here. *If* she got here. "She should be back by now. Are you *sure* she's not back?"

Lyle didn't even answer. He just turned and swam away.

Aaron took my hand, and we followed Lyle back toward the beach.

"Lyle, stop!" I called.

He was already out of the water, his tail turning back into legs. "What for?" he asked, his voice broken and cracked, as if it were full of splinters.

"It . . . it's not over yet. Please. Wait. Just for a while."

Lyle sighed. Then he held out his arms in a hopeless shrug. "OK." He sat on the sand. "I'll wait. What else is there for me to do?"

Mandy splashed into the waves. "You made it!" she screamed.

I hugged Mandy, told her how glad I was to be back. Then I dived back into the water to join Shona when we saw her arriving a few minutes later. I danced around in a happy circle with her and told her how scary it had been, but how good it felt to be safely back in one piece. I sat at the water's edge with Lyle, holding his hand, telling him not to give up, telling him Lowenna would be safe.

But I was lying as I did *all* of those things.

Inside, my heart was breaking. I'd failed. The one person I'd gone to collect hadn't made it back. How could we be happy about *any* of this?

It was almost pitch-black when Lyle got up and brushed sand off his legs.

"She's not coming," he said. "It's over. I'm going home."

As he turned to walk up the beach, I got up, too. "Wait!"

Lyle turned back.

I had to tell him. He was right. Lowenna had gone. It was obvious she hadn't made it, and I'd promised her that if she didn't come back, I'd pass on her message.

But how could I do that? How could I tell him about a daughter he had lost before he'd even laid eyes on her?

I opened my mouth to speak and was searching around for the worst words in the world when Mandy tugged at my arm. "Emily!"

"Hang on. I need to —"

"Emily!" This time it was Aaron. I turned back to them. They'd both stood up and were looking out to sea.

Mandy was pointing. "Look. Look!"

Lyle and I peered in the direction Mandy was pointing. It was hard to see anything out there on the dark-blue sea against the sky that was nearly black. But Mandy was right: there was something in the water.

Bright above the waves. Moving through the water. Nearly here. A person with red straggly hair, bright-green eyes that shone like a cat's against the dark sky — and a bundle in her arms.

"Lyle!" Her voice came across to us like a song being played on the wind. "My love!"

Lyle ran to the water so fast he almost fell to his knees. "Lowenna! Lowenna. Oh, my darling! You're alive! You're home!"

A second later, Lowenna had reached us. In the shallows of the water, Lyle threw his arms around her so hard it was as if he'd wrapped her in a giant blanket. They stayed like that for a moment, swaying in the water, arms tight around each other.

Then Lyle drew away. He looked down at the

bundle in her arms. At first sight, it could have been a bag made of seaweed and filled with findings from the ocean.

"What's this? Whose is it?" he asked as Lowenna reached down and held the bundle out to him.

"This," she said with a smile brighter than the moon that had begun to rise, "is our baby girl."

With a quick smile and a grateful nod in my direction, she passed the baby into his arms. "Daddy, meet your daughter, Atlanta Emily Waters."

We had about a minute of delirious happiness before we all felt it.

Something was happening. The ground was shaking. The sea was grumbling—waves grew as the swell pushed the tide higher up the beach.

"What's going on?" Mandy hissed.

"I don't know," I replied. "An earthquake?"

"We've never had an earthquake here on the island," Lyle said, folding his baby daughter more tightly into his arms.

Shona was at the water's edge, bobbing up and down as the waves hurled her around. "Look!" she said, pointing out toward the horizon.

I followed where she was pointing. Squinting into the darkness, I could see some kind of movement.

Black shapes diving through the surf. Dolphins! Lots of them. They were pulling something. It looked like . . .

"Neptune!" Aaron exclaimed.

Lowenna swung around to look. "What's *he* doing here?" she breathed.

As Neptune's chariot was pulled closer to the shore and the dolphins came to rest in the breaking waves, his figure was clearly visible against the night sky. He towered in his chariot, holding his trident in the air, the moonlight shining down on him like a spotlight on a stage.

Neptune ordered his dolphins away, then rose higher in his chariot and waved his trident. As he did, the waves died down and the earth stopped rumbling.

I tried to swallow. Tried to breathe normally. This wasn't good.

Before I could start to calculate exactly how much trouble I was going to be in *this* time, someone else appeared from the other side of the chariot. As he swam to the water's edge and pulled the chariot closer to the shore, I could see who it was.

So could someone else.

"Seth!" Shona swam over to him and was about to throw her arms around him when Neptune very ostentatiously cleared his throat. Not that Neptune does anything *un*-ostentatiously.

"Neptune has something he wants to say," Seth

announced in a formal tone I'd never heard him use before. I guess it was his work voice.

We all fell silent while we waited for Neptune to speak.

Eventually, in a calm, even, very un-Neptune-like voice, he said, "My young adviser here told me what you were attempting, and I wanted to see it for myself."

Seth told Neptune what we were doing?

He flashed a quick *I'm sorry* look over to us.

"I forced him to," Neptune went on. "I could tell he was concerned, worried. I do not need my staff being distracted by worries or concerns. I insisted he tell me. His honesty will be rewarded."

I couldn't blame Seth for telling him what was going on. When Neptune insists on something, you don't have a lot of choice about whether to do it or not. I knew that.

"No one has ever done this before," Neptune went on. "Not once. Not ever. It has been attempted, but never successfully. I had no reason to believe this occasion would be any different."

No one spoke. No one moved. We all just listened.

"Atlantis is one of the best-kept secrets in my kingdom, and those who work for it are among my most treasured staff," Neptune continued. "Which is why I decided to come here. My intention was to come to you to offer my condolences." He looked across at Lyle and Lowenna, his gaze falling on the baby. "I can see," he said, "that there was no need."

Then he did this weird thing with his face. I'm fairly sure I'd never seen him do it before, so it took a moment to realize exactly what it was. He was smiling! "Instead," he said, "we shall join you in a celebration. Tonight, take to your beds, your homes, settle back into your lives. Tomorrow, as a celebration and a reward for the bravery and expertise shown by all of you . . ."

At which point he half turned so he was looking directly at me. I gulped and tried to remember he was praising me, not punishing me. Then I did a weird kind of smile-thing back at him.

"I shall spend the day here with you. You have two days remaining of your trip, I believe?"

"That's right, Your Majesty," Shona said. "Thursday and Friday. We all leave Saturday morning."

"Then I shall spend the night preparing some treats for you. Tomorrow there shall be dolphin rides for all the Brightport children, voyages of discovery to the most secret caves in the area for the Shiprock class. And we will end the day with a banquet that I will instruct my personal staff to create and send over. We will make it the best day any geography trip has ever seen! How does that sound?"

How did it sound? It sounded amazing!

Lowenna edged into the water toward the chariot. "It sounds swishy, Your Majesty," she said. "Thank you!"

Neptune shuffled in his chariot. "Very well," he said. "You're welcome." He looked down at Seth. "Now, get me to my nearest palace and then you can come back and spend some time with your"— he glanced at Shona—"with your *friends*," he finished, emphasizing the word enough so that I could see Seth's cheeks burn even in the darkness.

As Neptune sat back down in his chariot, Seth grinned at Shona. "See you soon," he said.

She smiled back so brightly that the moon had a competitor for a moment.

"Come on, now," Neptune ordered in the loud booming voice that was much more like him. "I don't have all evening, you know."

With that, Seth swam back around, turning the chariot away from us. Neptune banged his trident against the front of the chariot and the dolphins reappeared.

A moment later, they were all gone.

I hugged Shona good-bye.

"See you tomorrow," she said. "I can't wait!"

"Me neither," I agreed. I could hardly believe

what had just happened. Any of it, in fact. I was pretty sure I wouldn't sleep much tonight.

"'Night, 'night, sweetheart," Shona said softly, looking at Atlanta. Atlanta Emily. The rest of us turned and headed up the beach.

"I thought she didn't have a name," I said shyly to Lowenna as Aaron and I walked back to Lyle and Lowenna's house with them, Lowenna and Lyle hand in hand, Lyle carrying his baby daughter in his other arm so lovingly it was as if he had waited all his life to hold her.

"She didn't," Lowenna replied with a soft smile. "But somewhere in the middle of that crazy portal, I knew what her name had to be. She was named for two things: first, the place she was born." She paused and touched my arm. "And second, for an incredibly strong, brave, and wonderful young person. If she grows up to be half as remarkable as you, she'll be able to achieve anything she wants."

"Her name is perfect," Lyle murmured as we walked.

I couldn't speak. I didn't even try.

We got back to our cabin and said our good-byes. Lyle, Lowenna, and Atlanta had a lot of catching up to do.

"We'll see you tomorrow," Lowenna said. Then she held me close and whispered in my ear, "Thank you for giving me my life back."

I held her tight. "You're welcome," I croaked.

"You coming in?" Mandy asked at the cabin door.

"Actually, I need to talk to Emily," Aaron said sharply before I had the chance to answer. "We'll be there in a bit."

"Cool." Mandy nudged my hip on her way in. "It's good to have you back, fish girl," she said. "Had me worried for a bit there."

I nudged her back. "It's good to be here," I said with a smile.

Aaron led the way. "Come on," he said. "Let's go for a walk. There's something I have to tell you."

We walked along the road that led to Deep Blue Bay. My stomach was in jitters — not just because of Neptune's visit but also because of Aaron wanting to talk. After all those moments when he'd brushed me off in one way or another — and what Lyle had told me about Aaron not feeling the same as me — I wasn't sure I *wanted* to talk. What if he was planning to break up with me? I didn't think I could handle it if a day like this ended like *that*.

When we got there, Aaron jumped up onto one of the big, smooth boulders and reached down to help me up.

I sat next to him. It was the same spot where

we'd sat before trekking off along the path that had led us to the chair—the start of this whole crazy, scary, amazing adventure.

"So," I said nervously, "why are we here? What did you want to tell me?"

Aaron shifted so he was facing me. A nearly full moon was still climbing high into the sky, its white light reaching across the sea like a searchlight, just bright enough for me to see his face.

He took both of my hands in his. "Look, there's something I need to say," he began.

No! He *was* going to break up with me. I could tell by the way he was holding my hands like he felt sorry for me, like he wanted to make it easier on me.

"I've been wanting to tell you for a while now," he went on.

I tried to resign myself to what was coming.

"I guess the moment hasn't been right," he continued. "But now it is, and I can't stop myself any longer." Aaron took a breath, then looked me straight in the eyes.

Here it comes, I thought. *The big breakup speech.*

And then he said, "Emily Windsnap, I love you."

What?

"What did you say?" I asked, like an idiot.

Aaron laughed. "I said I love you," he repeated.

He loved me! *That* was why he wasn't between

states. Not because he didn't even like me—but because he loved me! And Lyle knew it before I did!

His words were like a switch. I know it sounds cheesy, but it felt as if they lit up something inside me—clicked something into place. Made everything right.

And it was safe for me now, too. I didn't have to be between states. I could let myself feel the feelings I'd been holding back for the last few days.

I smiled at him. "I'm so glad," I said. "Because I love you, too."

The moon had risen higher in the sky. It shone a spotlight onto a round patch of sea in the bay below us. Beyond that patch, the ocean was in darkness. *There are so many mysteries out there,* I thought as I rested my head on Aaron's shoulder and snuggled in closer to him. So much was unknown; there was so much darkness, fear, danger.

As I looked up, the first star came out. Mom always said that if you make a wish on the first star you see at night, you can get anything you want.

I smiled to myself as more and more stars began to emerge and Aaron held me close.

I had no need for wishes. They had already come true.

Epilogue

The janitor was locking up at the Prosper Vacations headquarters when a radio crackled into life in the main office.

Probably nothing, he thought. Then he spotted the radar and saw a red dot flashing. He didn't know much about radar, but there'd been a lot of talk in the office that week about a missing ship: *Prosperous II.*

The ship had disappeared the previous Friday. The company had managed to keep the incident out of the public eye, as there'd been no reports of an accident. One day it had been on the radar; the next, it had gone. What if this was that ship?

Maybe he should take the call.

The janitor crept into the office and switched on the light.

"Prosper Vacations HQ, Prosper Vacations HQ, this is *Prosperous II*. *Prosperous II*. Do you read me? Over."

The janitor picked up a radio from its cradle on the desk. He knew how they worked. He'd seen others use them. "I read you," he said carefully. "Um. Over."

The voice that came through was joyful. "Prosper Vacations HQ, am I glad to hear you! This is the captain of *Prosperous II*. I would like to apologize for going off the map while we took a brief detour. Over."

The janitor could hardly believe his ears. "I . . . er . . . that's great news," he replied eventually. "Are you all safe and well? Over."

"Affirmative. All passengers are on board, safe, healthy, and looking forward to going home. I repeat, we are on our way home. Please tell our families we will see them soon! This is *Prosperous II* out."

The janitor had to hold the radio away from his ear. As the captain had spoken, the cheers and whoops in the background had almost deafened him. "Well, Captain, I'm very pleased to hear that," he said after rubbing his ear. "We wish you a safe homeward journey, and we're very glad to have you back. We will of course inform your families. Um, this is HQ out."

As he put the radio back in its cradle, the janitor looked around for a piece of paper so he could leave a note for his boss. Then he changed his mind. News like this couldn't wait till morning.

He searched the files for the family lists—and then he started to make the calls himself. His wife would understand his being home late when he told her what he'd been doing.

The first call was answered on the third ring. "Hello?" It was a woman's voice.

The janitor cleared his throat. "Is this Olivia Mason?" he asked.

"Yes, that's me," the voice replied. "Who's this?"

The janitor sat a little straighter in his chair and spoke as clearly and as formally as he could. "Mrs. Mason, I've got some wonderful news . . ."

And while the janitor sat in a small office making happy phone calls, and a boy and a girl huddled together on a headland, and a group of passengers partied as they made their way home—inside a small house, a man sat in front of a warm, crackling fire, his wife in his arms beside him, their baby snuggled on his lap.

As they watched her miraculous little face, she wriggled and gurgled. Then she opened her eyes, and, for the first time in her tiny little life, looked up at her parents, and smiled.